By Mitchell Wynne

Written by Mitchell Wynne

Edited by Tevin Geter

Book cover by Ambrojah

Philippians 4:13

I can do all things through Christ who strengthens me.

Table of Contents

PROLOGUE

1, 2, 3, 4, 5, ready or not, here I come, dead or alive.

This was the cadence Miteous Reese called out from the nook underneath the slide at an elementary school on the westside of Omaha, Nebraska, where the air seemed to be of better quality, along with everything else built by investors on that side of town. That's why his mother sent him and his siblings on an hour-long bus ride out there every morning in the first place.

It had become the norm that whenever Miteous wanted to play, he was automatically chosen to be "it," decided by most kids who played because Miteous was the fastest kid in the entire school. And he was only in kindergarten. Not to mention, this school went all the way up to fourth grade.

He was genetically predisposed to be an all-around athlete thanks to his father's DNA. Ricardo "The Roadrunner" Reese Sr. had been one of the state's most talented running backs coming out of high school in the eighties. But being misguided and lazy in school ended up being his downfall, and he never got the chance to pursue his dreams of going to the NFL.

Miteous knew that if he opted out of being "it" during recess, he wouldn't feel like part of the game because nobody was even going to bother chasing someone, they knew they couldn't catch. It was like trying to catch the wind. It just wasn't going to happen.

After scanning the crowded blacktop like a hawk looking for prey, he finally decided to chase the prettiest girl in class, Veronica Taylor. Not only because he was attracted to her, but also because he couldn't pass up the opportunity to try and cop a quick feel during their little game. One she had already granted him full permission to play.

He knew how much she liked the attention and couldn't help but take advantage of both situations especially while he had the power of the tag to make his move.

Just as he was about to approach Veronica and slap her on the backside, his legs tangled up. He almost did a full front flip, landing face-first in the dirt. But before his face hit the gravel, he stuck out his arm to break the fall. His left hand hit the ground first, snapping his wrist completely on impact, though he hadn't realized that part yet, nor the cause of it all.

Heartbeat racing. Adrenaline rushing. Eyesight blurry.

Miteous was eventually able to get his bearings back and rolled over onto his back, trying to sit up so he could assess the damage and figure out what the hell just happened.

He'd run way faster, for far longer, in much worse terrain, and he prided himself on his superior kinesthetic intelligence. So how could he have tripped over his own two feet like Humpty Dumpty without even a pebble in sight?

As he sat there looking around, a small crowd had formed around him. He stared at several familiar faces, some with smirks, others with looks of deep concern. But he noticed two things that were off.

One was this kid standing a little too close for comfort, someone he'd never seen before joining in their game. The second was the look on Veronica's face. She stood out from the rest because of the wild expression she had, one of both disgust and surprise.

Miteous was taken aback by it. He hadn't even tagged her on the bottom yet like he'd intended, so why was she looking at him like he had?

Then, as soon as he went to get back on his feet to dust himself off, he started noticing a real stiffness and sharp pains shooting up his left arm. That's when he finally realized the reason for the looks he'd been getting.

His left wrist had been completely bent into an S-shape, like a snake in motion. Even he couldn't help but stare at it in disgust.

After becoming fully aware of the damage, that's when he started to feel completely engulfed in pain. But he didn't cry in front of everyone because Miteous was just that tough when it came to managing his emotions, even early on.

While he was still trying to assess the whole situation play-by-play, recess was called over. Miteous told his teacher about his injury and was taken to the nurse's office. His parents were contacted and came to pick him up. Then he was taken to the emergency room, where he got a cast put on and received special attention from the female doctors.

But for the rest of that day, Miteous kept going over everything that had happened in his head. And he couldn't stop thinking about that unfamiliar face he'd seen right after falling.

Who the hell was that kid? he wondered.

And why was he the first person I noticed after I came to?

He didn't know. But the next day at school, he planned on getting to the bottom of it.

When Miteous returned the next day, now sporting a freshly wrapped cast, he got a bunch of special attention from the other kids. Every girl in his class wanted to sign it in their own special way.

But all Miteous could think about was recess.

He needed answers.

Time moved in slow motion that day. When recess was finally called, he was the first one out there. It didn't take long before the blacktop was filled with all the other kindergartners, just like always.

But this time, Miteous took a vantage point. He scanned the crowd with a watchful eye and a look that could kill.

He wasn't the only one trying to get the drop, though.

He quickly spun around when he heard an unfamiliar voice.

"Wassup foo? U lookin' for me, ain't chu?"

When he turned around, he was staring face to face with his new adversary.

As Miteous looked the kid up and down, he was caught off guard by his bold attitude and aggressive demeanor. It was a lot like himself. He couldn't help but laugh a little at the irony.

Then he replied, "So that was you the other day that had somethin' to do with' me fallin', huh? But why, man? What I do to you? I ain't never even played with you before. What's yo' name?"

The kid took this as a sign of weakness. He stepped closer, looked Miteous in the eye, stuck his chest out a bit, and said, "My name TayVaughn Kelly, and I saw u 'bouta make a move on my girl, so I made my move on u."

Miteous was surprised by this and replied, "Who? Veronica? Man, I ain't trippin' over no female here, dude, and if u knew what I know, u wouldn't be either. So, check this out, how 'bout we team up in tag, keep the 'it' between us? That way, we can chase all the girls every day."

TayVaughn had never thought about it like that. It quickly changed his whole demeanor and facial expression.

Right then and there, he gained a different type of respect for Miteous. He knew in his heart he had just found a friend for life.

Once Miteous noticed the change in his energy, he stuck out his hand, calling a truce to their dispute. It was quickly met with the same enthusiasm.

And in that moment, the bond was built.

Before recess ended and the two friends parted ways, Miteous smiled sinisterly at his new friend and said, "Ay doe! U know after my wrist heals up, I'ma beat that ass still, don't chu?"

Now it was Tay's turn to laugh. Then he nodded in agreement and said he'd be ready.

They stared each other down, then both started laughing as they returned to their separate classes.

From that point on, the two were as thick as thieves, meeting up every day at recess until the end of kindergarten, chasing all the girls they liked together.

CHAPTER 1

Growing up on the northeast side of Omaha in a two-parent household in a middle-class neighborhood, where crime occurred but not as rampantly as in other parts of the city, Miteous Dwayne Reese had a lot more shelter from the nonsense than most kids down North back then.

Even if he didn't know or appreciate the safe space he'd been provided to grow up in, it could've been a lot worse. Especially in a conservative state filled with prejudice and bias against its minorities.

That same bias had caused cultural defects that left many of its African American natives too miseducated and broken to fully utilize the resources they needed to survive the systematic aftershocks of the crack epidemic and the so-called war on drugs and crime. Trying to raise the next generation with all the essentials they needed to succeed, most from single-parent homes and government-assisted living, was a battle.

But not Miteous.

He had it all: both biological parents, and both came from good stock. Ricardo Reese Sr. and Lonica Reese loved, clothed, and taught him exactly who he was and where he came from his entire life, so the world couldn't define it for him.

They instilled in him confidence, a strong will, loyalty, and a hard work ethic. And they demonstrated those values in their own lives and marriage from the time he was young.

They didn't smoke or drink, and they prioritized their children over everything else, giving them their time and attention, creating a real hospitable home to grow up in.

Lonica Reese was an educator for over 15 years. Ricardo Reese Sr. worked hard labor jobs and legit side hustles since he was 18, landscaping, dog breeding, selling used cars, just to name a few.

They were also a God-fearing family and attended service nearly every Sunday with Miteous and his four siblings: Ricardo Jr., Luther, Tychia, and Engcong. All had the same mother and father, ensuring they grew up with enriched spirits, deep morals, and a strong sense of who God was.

So, whatever their parents couldn't teach, show, or provide, God could, if they kept their faith in Him. No matter where their individual journeys took them, He would always be there... even if they weren't.

But you can lead a horse to water, you can't make it drink.

Miteous Reese had his own ideals and agenda when it came to scripting his life. He was what the church-going folks called the black sheep of the family. He was always getting into trouble and stirring up strife, no matter where he went or who was around.

From the time he was young, he was a real rambunctious soul.

No matter how many times he got rebuked for his bad attitude and wicked ways, he never made up his mind to turn over a new leaf in life. And the older he got, the worse he became. The more trouble seemed to find him.

Some would say what Miteous needed was a positive male role model his own age because at that tender stage in life, a child's biggest influences are his peers.

But his mother had other ideas in mind.

When beating the black off him didn't work, she tried having him baptized. The deacons at church would lay hands on him and pray over him regularly. But he always seemed to go right back to his old ways, opting to learn his lessons the hard way.

Noticing the path their son was headed down if he didn't make major adjustments early on, and seeing his natural tendency for violence, aggression, and meddling, they came up with the perfect solution: channel all that raw emotion and energy into sports.

They put him in every sport they could afford from the time he was six or seven years old.

During the winter, it was wrestling, where he learned discipline, balance, and how to channel his aggression. He also learned how to stand alone on and off the mat.

He saw how closely the sport mirrored life. You had to use 80% of your mental and only 20% of your physical to dominate your opponent.

But he'd still get in trouble for using those skills off the mat more than on it. That led to coaches disciplining him by matching him up with more experienced wrestlers who would repeatedly get the best of him. Not just to toughen him up, but to teach him humility.

But Miteous still never learned. He just became more aggressive, only now in a more controlled way.

In the spring, they tried martial arts, since he idolized Bruce Lee. The discipline taught inner peace and how to connect the mind with the body's movements.

But Miteous often challenged his instructors. His bad technique and slick remarks frustrated them so much, they eventually gave his parents their money back and dismissed him.

Then he got into track and field, where he excelled, making it all the way to the Junior Olympics at just eight years old. But once those eight weeks were over, he went right back to his old ways, only now in excellent shape.

Finally, in the fall, they signed him up for football, and that's where he found the right channel. The one thing he was most passionate about. Achieving success in that was the only thing worth staying out of trouble for. And that's when it all started happening.

> *"Like the waves of the sea are the ways of fate.*
> *As we voyage along through life,*
> *'Tis the set of the soul which decides its goal,*
> *And not the calm or the strife."*
> – Ella Wheeler Wilcox

Living in a world where information is key and knowledge with understanding is power, TayVaughn Mason Kelly grew up exposed to the game early. He was taught all the rudimentary life skills it took to survive in the Underworld, and he quickly got used to it.

Raised in a guttural trench on the far north end of Omaha, where it wasn't safe to walk the streets alone at night or leave anything outside, you'd miss, unless it was within arm's reach, TayVaughn's upbringing was as rough as it gets.

As his mother's only child, by miracle and accident, he was what most would consider a lost cause or a delinquent. He grew up in government-assisted housing, a Section 8 project where state workers dictated the terms and conditions of your living arrangements. There was no sense of discipline or structure.

With a mother on drugs and a father he never met, Tay started his criminal career early.

Having a mom that changed men like underwear gave Tay all kinds of opportunities for quick and easy come ups. He started off pickpocketing her new dudes for money, sometimes right after late-night escapades with his mother, catching them slipping in drug-induced comas, scavenging whatever he could.

Whether it was meals, new threads, drug money, jewelry, or even weapons, he took it all. And every time, his mother took the blame and the beatings. She'd grown used to both in her condition and lifestyle.

He moved on to stealing from convenience and grocery stores, supporting both his hunger and his mom's habit. Her instructions for survival became second nature. What started out as surviving quickly escalated to more serious crimes for bigger gains as he got older.

And once he got good at it, he became addicted to the rush of getting away with it. His profitable scams had him hooked.

TayVaughn's only sense of normalcy was school. That's where he confided in the only person he trusted, his best friend in the world, Miteous, who had been down with him since kindergarten.

Now that they were in high school, Tay noticed a lot of things were starting to change with his body and mind. He may not have been the smartest kid in school, and he didn't do as well as Miteous academically, but he was far from a dropout. And there weren't too many kids his age with better street sense than him, that was for sure.

Growing up in a neighborhood where a lot of other urban kids did too give Tay notoriety among his peers, and Miteous too, because of how close they were.

Then, walking home from school one day, Tay reached a crossroads in life that would change the course of his fate forever.

After several competitive seasons of little league football, where he developed in skill, size, and strength, Miteous had become the talk of the town. With an older brother and a dad who had been talented athletes before him, he already had the bloodline and the reputation. He was seen as a high school hopeful, even with state championship potential.

Throughout the years, he'd maintained a close friendship with TayVaughn. Tay would often spend the night on weekends when Miteous didn't have a game or school event, and almost every day during the summer when he wasn't training or practicing.

But their time together became a quiet threat to Miteous's growth, whether he realized it or not.

They would often go out and steal from stores, roam the neighborhood, stir up mischief, and link with girls. That time together, even though it was more destructive than constructive, gave TayVaughn an escape from his everyday life.

But it also started having a negative influence on Miteous.

Tay's crime stories and secrets fed into a hunger for attention and recognition. The more time Miteous spent around him, the more toxic that influence became.

Not to mention, Miteous had way more to lose than he did to gain from indulging in petty crimes with his friend. But he couldn't shake the euphoric feeling he got every time he pulled something off, every time he got over on someone and made some quick cash.

Eventually, he started planning out his own licks. He'd include Tay not just because he needed a partner, but because he knew Tay needed it more than he did.

As the years went on, Miteous started feeling like he was getting the best of both worlds. He became more and more obsessed with coming up in the game, a game that belonged to those criminally bent on making victims out of consumers.

But we all reap what we sow. And the devil will give you all the right tools to destroy yourself in the end.

Miteous learned that the hard way.

CHAPTER 2

"Hey Sammy, how's my favorite nephew?" Bossman Booker called out from the back of the pawn shop he owned, located in downtown Omaha. He bought, sold, and loan-sharked all types of valuables he felt were worth his time, anything he could flip for profit, no questions asked.

When he heard the bell jingle above the door frame, signaling someone had entered, he instinctively checked the monitors connected to the security cameras he had placed all around the shop. That was all the protection he needed, besides his personalized .357 Magnum.

He noticed his sister's oldest son stepping inside.

Samuel Davis, known to his peers as Sammy D, was now in high school and one of the state's most talked-about linebackers in the metro. He'd been getting good grades most of his life, only struggling when his mom broke the news that his father had been killed in a car accident a few years back.

After that, Booker had stepped up and played a major role in the boy's life, someone Sammy both admired and revered. Even though Booker pushed a lot of weight in the community, making it a rougher environment to grow up in, Sammy still looked up to him as a role model.

"Wassup, Unc," said Sammy D, embracing him with love as he walked up. "Still checkin' dem monitors every five minutes, ain't chu? That's how you knew it was me, huh?"

Laughing lightheartedly and getting straight down to business like he'd taught him, Booker said, "You know what brought me by the shop today? I heard Moms on the phone witchu last night."

He rubbed his hands together like he was trying to warm them up, referring to the quarterly update she'd given him about his grades. They were usually straight A's, and Sammy always got rewarded heavily for it.

"Yeah, she told me. You did yo' thang, that's what I like to hear. Keep it up and I'ma have to give you the shop on consignment, man, you be breakin' me," Booker said jokingly. "Nah but real shit though, Sam, I'm proud of you, dawg. Keep handlin' business, boy, and you gon' make it. Watch what I tell you. Yo' pops would be proud of you too, no doubt. But here, doe,"

He handed his nephew two fresh, crispy blue faces, then started smiling.

"Unless you want some store credit instead this time."

That made Sammy D bust out laughing. He only stopped to say, "Man, everybody know half this crap ain't real, and the other half some crackhead done stole to get high. And people still lookin' for it. No offense though, Unc, but I'm coo."

Laughing at his nephew's quick wit, Booker said casually, "None taken. And boy, you know you too smart for yo' own damn good sometimes, though, don't chu?"

19

But then he shifted gears.

"On a serious note, nephew, I do got some extra ends for you too if you send anybody my way with some nice merch they tryin' to get rid of, but they can't move it nowhere else. If you pickin' up on what I'm layin' down, just tell 'em to come through in yo' name and I got chu. You know where I'll be at."

Sammy D shook his head, told his uncle he'd keep an eye out, said his farewells, and exited the shop to go about his day.

Booker returned to the back to get started on his work. The day was just beginning, and he had to prepare for whatever unpredictable bullshit came with running a pawn shop, especially on this side of town, where the crackheads stayed creepin on a come up at all hours.

It wasn't long after he got back to taking inventory that the bell above the door chimed again.

In walked one of his favorite smokers, who looked like he'd seen better days.

Disheveled, musty, hair wild, no shave or shower in weeks, he stomped into the shop like he owned it and demanded to see Booker right away.

"Aye, muthafucka! I know yo' cheap ass 'round here somewhere. Now bring yo' monkey ass out here and holla at cha boy so I can be on my way!" yelled Fleewell Jones, the local neighborhood thief, burglar, and now handyman, calling out from the main corridor.

He'd been known as Fleewell long before Booker ever met him. The name came from his reputation for dodging police during foot chases since the '80s, back when he first started smoking and robbing his fellow townsfolk to support his habit.

"Man, what chu want now? Shit! You know I stay busy 'round here. You betta have somethin' expensive for me today, doin' all that goddamn yellin' in my shop this mornin'. So, let's see the goods," Booker barked as he came out from the back, irritation all over his face.

He had just finished loading his .357 Magnum, something he always brought up front and placed under the counter whenever a customer like Fleewell came through. Just in case.

It had become second nature at this point.

He'd already spotted Fleewell's bowlegged walk on one of the monitors and had been anticipating his arrival.

Booker approached the counter and discreetly slid the gun underneath, ready for whatever.

Fleewell jumped right in.

"You know Fleewell keeps the best for sale, baby. Now gon' break me off a lil' some for these," he snapped, pulling out two gold rope chains from his pocket. Then a third, this one diamond-encrusted with a nice, thick clasp that read 24k. At first glance, it looked like a real Cuban link.

He laid all three chains on the counter and just stood there scratching at his skin, scanning the shop with a veteran crook's eye, the kind that comes from years of ill behavior.

Booker was momentarily distracted by the merchandise. The quality was better than usual, and he couldn't tell if it was fake or not just by looking. Still, he stayed on code.

"Now you know I don't keep no dope in here, ol' skoo. But if everything checks out, I'ma call Tony and Mike to take care of you, like always. Just wait right here, I'll be right back."

Forgetting his magnifier and gold tester in the back, Booker was eager to check the chains out, already running numbers in his head if they turned out to be the real deal.

He left Fleewell standing there, completely forgetting about the loaded pistol he'd tucked under the counter just moments before.

But when Booker came back with the bad news, after discovering the chains were fake, he was completely flabbergasted.

There wasn't a soul in sight. It was like Fleewell had vanished into thin air like Houdini.

Booker couldn't believe it. He hadn't even heard the bell jingle on the way out.

Finally coming to grips with what had just happened, he realized he'd gotten duped. The experienced doper had got him. He was mad at himself for letting his greed cloud his instincts, again.

Frustrated, he turned to check the surveillance footage to assess the damage. But before heading to the back, he reached under the counter to grab his pistol first.

That's when he discovered it wasn't there anymore either.

He was furious.

Instantly heated like a furnace, raging like a bull, he pulled out his cellphone and couldn't dial fast enough, calling up his two main hitters, hustlers, and loyal street soldiers: Tony and Mike.

Even in the Underworld, laws govern all events, and there's always a hierarchy. And with Booker being one of the top dogs in his organization, he had individuals under him who carried out whatever needed to be done so operations could keep running smoothly, and so the king on the chessboard, which was him, always stayed in a protected position of power.

Whether it was having people killed who got in the way of his business, extorting growing organizations not yet as powerful as his, taking a cut of their hustle in the process, or just day-to-day oversight of the trap spots he had set up across the city, Booker moved his products through it all.

And if he was the General, then Tony and Mike were his Captains. Each had their own lieutenants, underbosses, and foot soldiers.

But in this dog-eat-dog style of living, you gotta be real meticulous about who you let eat at your table. Because in some cases, when you feed wild animals... they'll eat you too.

Tony and Mike were always together, so much so that everybody in town who knew them rarely saw one without the other, no matter where they were or what was going on. That alone made them a force in the streets.

They weren't the sharpest knives in the drawer, but two minds were always better than one, especially when they

23

were motivated, on the same page, and able to perform at the same high level as they could.

They had an indestructible will when it came to their pursuit of power and wealth. Crude determination. An errand purpose. But no matter how locked in you are, failure comes for everyone eventually.

They were cruising the city, showing off Tony's brand-new Benz. He had just scooped up Mike and they were headed toward one of the traps, making their usual rounds. The day had just begun.

That's when Tony's phone rang.

He recognized the number instantly, he never saved it in his contacts, for discretion. Answered it after the second ring.

"Bossman, talk to me," he said, already knowing it was Booker. If he was calling, it meant there was a situation he wanted handled personally.

Booker's voice came through the receiver, tight with rage.

"Ay man, y'all seen that muthafucka Fleewell today? 'Cause I need y'all to grab him, take him for a rough ride, then bring him to me. This muthafucka must think shit sweet around here or somethin'."

A *rough ride* meant bound, tossed in the trunk, no talking.

He filled them in on what had gone down at the pawn shop and warned them to be careful. Fleewell had stolen his favorite piece, his custom .357, which he named *Alexandra*.

Still holding their cards close, Tony and Mike agreed to handle it. Then they hung up.

Booker rushed to the back to pull the security footage and discovered exactly what was taken, and how it was done.

First, he watched himself, rushing to the back with the chains, not even worried about Fleewell anymore.

That's when the show began.

Fleewell immediately went to work. Pulled out a piece of gum, a pair of gloves, and a little hygiene baggie from his pocket. Then he jumped behind the counter with the agility of an athlete.

He grabbed a couple high-priced pieces of jewelry and stuffed them in the baggie.

Looked down. Spotted the gun.

Snatched it.

Hopped back over the counter. Ran to the door. Stuck the gum inside the bell, that's why Booker never heard it chime.

Then he bolted down the street like an Olympic sprinter, gone, completely off-camera, before Booker ever made it back up front.

After watching the tape a few times, Booker couldn't shake the feeling that he'd been set up.

The question of *why* and *by who* drove him mad. Who would even try him like that? And what was their endgame, other than a closed casket, once he got his answers?

Hell, if Fleewell was already risking his life stealing from a man of Booker's magnitude, why not press his luck and take the money too?

It didn't sit right.

The more Booker thought about it, the more paranoid he became. That's when the conspiracy started to formulate in the back of his head.

And slowly, he began to realize exactly who the real culprits were behind the staged heist.

Whether or not he could prove it was still up in the air.

But one thing he knew for sure, somebody in his organization could no longer be trusted.

Or *people*...

CHAPTER 3

It started off like any other school day. Everything felt routine, same rhythm, same energy, except something was off. Miteous couldn't shake the eerie feeling hanging in the air, like an invisible presence was watching him.

Just as he started to get on his feet to stretch out the stiffness from a good night's sleep, he smelled breakfast in the air, bacon, eggs, sausages, and pancakes. His favorite.

Then his door flew open.

"Woke up this morning with my mind, and it stayed on Jesus! Hallelujah, hallelujah, halleluuujah!"

It was his mom, Lonica Reese, singing loud as hell with a plate in her hand. She set it on his computer desk and called him by his full name, telling him he better get a move on if he wanted a ride on her way to work.

He thanked her as nicely as he could, still annoyed by her loud antics and terrible singing disturbing his peace of mind. At that moment, he thought he'd rather have had a real-life rooster cock-a-doodle-dooing outside his window as an alarm clock, it would've been much more subtle.

Still, he knew he was her favorite, so he took the good with the bad.

Either way, he was grateful. The meal was solid, and Pops was putting it down too, serving breakfast like royalty.

He devoured it, got dressed, washed his face, brushed his teeth, and made it to school on time. He even had enough time left before first period to meet up with Tay and get all the wild updates from his drama-filled life.

The day was going smooth, until fourth period study hall.

After finishing his work early so he wouldn't have to do it at home, Miteous started talking to this girl he liked, Tasha Tayor. She liked him too. They were vibing, making plans for the weekend, trying to agree on bringing a plus-one so her and her homegirl could hang with him and Tay. Maybe hit the mall or catch a movie and get to know each other better outside of school.

That's when some Mexican dude sitting behind them started hating, rudely jumping into their conversation.

"Ay foo, I'm tryna concentrate, homie. Take that shit somewhere else, Cupid," he said with attitude.

Miteous took it as disrespect, but didn't want to feed into the banter since he was making progress with Tasha. He turned around and said, "Well try harder then, foo. Can't chu see grown folks talkin', homie?"

Then he turned right back to Tasha, apologized for the interruption, and picked up where he left off.

But that had the Mexican dude spicy, like sriracha.

He kicked the back of Miteous' chair and said, "Pinche Mayate."

Now, Miteous wasn't the smartest kid in the world, and he damn sure wasn't bilingual, but he recognized the word *nigger* in any language.

And just like that, it was go time.

Excusing himself from the convo, Miteous turned all the way around in his seat, locked eyes with the dude, and said calmly, "Listen, homie, I don't know what the fuck yo' problem is today, but I got yo' solution waitin' on you outside after skoo. How 'bout that?"

The Mexican dude just chuckled arrogantly and said, "How 'bout it then, foo?"

After fourth period, Miteous told Tay what was up. Tay, more hyped than anything, said he'd be there to back him up. Then they went about the rest of the day like normal, but everybody who was in that class already knew what time it was.

By the end of the school day, the whole building was buzzing about the fight.

Miteous and Tay, being who they were, leaned into the attention like they were hired by Don King. They started promoting it, capitalizing off the hype, especially from all the girls who couldn't resist a bad boy.

So, when the bell rang, a crowd formed right out front of the school. It looked like a mini–Times Square during a special event.

When Miteous and Tay showed up at the agreed-upon location, they weren't surprised to see the Mexican dude waiting, posted with his own little entourage.

Tay, acting as the mediator-slash-referee, told everyone the rules were simple:

"If anybody else jump in or try to break it up, they gettin' they ass beat too."

And that's when Miteous stepped forward.

He walked right up to the dude he'd been into it with earlier and, right on cue, swung a hard, clean right straight to his jaw, no talking, no warning, just punches in bunches, fueled by rage.

By the time Miteous stepped out of his attack zone, the Mexican was done. Annihilated. No more malice, no more disrespect, just a dude offering a sincere apology for any misunderstanding they might've had.

But for every cause, there's an effect.

Even though Miteous got his point across, it caught the attention of security, then the principal. And that got him suspended from school for a week.

And later that night? His ass got effectively kicked again, by his father.

Meanwhile, tides weren't just turning in Miteous's life... but in TayVaughn's too.

After school security hauled Miteous off to the principal's office, Tay went on his way, starting his long journey home.

He'd missed his usual ride to stay behind for Miteous, so he had to walk, cutting through shortcuts, trying to get back to the projects before dark.

That's when he heard sirens.

A few blocks away. Closing in fast. Headed in the same direction he was.

Less than ten minutes later, he spotted the local neighborhood crackhead, Fleewell Jones, running down an alley. Dude had a flatscreen TV under one arm like a football and was charging downfield like he just broke the line of scrimmage, headed for a touchdown.

Three out-of-shape cops were behind him in hot pursuit, about twenty yards back and losing steam.

Tay, naturally curious, found a good vantage point to watch how it all played out. Especially since Fleewell was running straight toward him anyway.

As the distance closed between them, Fleewell saw an opportunity to gain some ground. He ditched the TV and everything else he had on him behind a big dumpster. Tay, about ten feet away and hidden, watched as Fleewell changed direction, leading the cops away from his stash.

Then he dashed through some houses, hopped two privacy fences, and instantly widened the gap between himself and the cops.

Tay couldn't help but respect it. Fleewell really lived up to his name.

Once they were all out of sight, Tay stepped out of hiding and went straight to the dumpster.

Time to take advantage.

Right next to the 30-inch flatscreen, which looked a lot bigger in Fleewell's frail arms, were two jewelry boxes. One had a pair of real diamond studs. The other held a diamond-encrusted tennis bracelet that had to be worth at least a couple thousand.

He grabbed them and stuffed them in his pockets. Then bent down to lift the TV with both hands, tilting it upright.

That's when he made his second discovery.

Underneath the TV was a brand-new, chrome-plated .357 Magnum.

TayVaughn lit up like a Christmas tree. He was so hyped, he almost walked away and left the TV behind just to avoid drawing attention to himself.

But since he was only a few blocks from his spot, he grabbed everything and headed home.

He'd found weapons before, usually on his mom's new dudes, but never a gun.

This was different.

This felt like graduation into the big leagues.

And it was...

A week flew by since Miteous had been kicked out of school and grounded from going anywhere. So, when he finally got to go back, he was excited, mainly to catch up with his boy so they could bask in his victory together over his adversary and see how many girls were jocking him because of the way he handled business.

But as soon as he got to school the day after his suspension was over, he could tell something had changed with Tay. He had a totally different demeanor, attitude, and swagger.

Curious, Miteous asked, "Wassup, bro? What gotchu feelin' like a million bucks?"

He approached Tay and embraced him with their own special handshake; one they'd been doing since kindergarten.

Still playing, Miteous kept joking, "I know you ain't gettin' no pussy, cause you don't even like girls."

"That ain't what yo' girl was sayin' last night, foo," Tay fired back without missing a beat.

The two started fake shadowboxing in the hallway. Tay, in a seemingly good mood, suddenly turned serious.

"Nah bro, on some real shit though, there's been some new developments, and I got somethin' I really need to show you, ASAP. Fuck my fourth period science, man. Let's get outta here real quick," Tay said.

Miteous, only having a study period, replied, "Man, I can't. Mom dukes be checkin' a nigga's attendance and shit."

Tay, always quick and cunning, said, "Just go in, fake a stomachache, and I'ma meet you out front."

By this point, Miteous was too curious. He didn't want to let his friend, who he considered his brother, down. So, he agreed, and they both headed to their classes.

Everything is running smoothly. Operation going accordingly.

Miteous made it out front, expecting Tay to pop out from somewhere playing. But there wasn't a soul in sight. Frustrated and confused, he turned back toward the building, thinking he might as well go back inside to study hall.

Then he heard a car horn honking excessively from the parking lot.

He turned around and was completely caught off guard.

Tay was behind the wheel of a beat-up old Mazda.

"Come on, nigga! Shit, let's get outta here!" Tay yelled out the window, flashing a Colgate smile.

Not wanting to look scary, Miteous walked to the passenger side and hopped in, but the questions started flying right away.

"Man, whose shit is this?" was his first one.

"Mines… for now," Tay said casually, then broke it down.

He told him how he'd come across the car a few days back, running outside some old lady's house. It had the keys still in it, and he'd just decided to hop in and take it. Drove off laughing the whole time, like it was a joke.

Miteous shook his head. "What else you been up to, dude? Cuz this ain't even what you normally do."

That's when Tay coldly replied, "Yeah… well somethin' changed."

Just as he said that, they pulled into the driveway of a house they'd never been to before.

Miteous couldn't help but question everything now. "And whose house is this?"

Tay killed the engine, smiled again, and said, "It's ours, for now. Come on."

He hopped out. Intrigued, Miteous followed.

They walked around to the back of a boarded-up residence that looked abandoned. It wasn't far from the school. As they approached the back entrance, which Tay had clearly broken into, Miteous could tell he'd been here multiple times before.

Inside, they climbed a couple sets of stairs up to the attic. Tay stepped carefully on the old wooden floorboards until he found the one he was looking for. He lifted it and revealed something wrapped in a cloth.

He unfolded it quickly, and there it was. A chrome revolver.

"And this ain't it either, bro. Check these out," Tay said.

Reaching back down into the hole under the floor, he came back out with two jewelry boxes and showed them to Miteous.

Even though he was impressed by Tay's recent come up, he still had to ask, "So… who did you rob for all this?"

That's when Tay filled him in, everything that had gone down last week after they'd parted ways.

After Tay's revelations and their little renegade rendezvous, Miteous returned to school like he'd never left. But he had a lot to think about.

Lucky for him, his suspension came before football season started. Still, he couldn't stop thinking about his future, how much of it he was willing to keep putting at risk by indulging in this lifestyle with his best friend, who seemed to be spiraling deeper by the day.

In this life, man is as he thinketh.

And then, when presented with choices, as he doeth.

In that moment, Miteous decided to get his life back on track. Focus on football. Focus on the dream.

But it doesn't take long to get thrown off your path when you're not fully committed to it.

And you always end up finding exactly what you're looking for…

It wasn't long before TayVaughn's whole way of thinking had completely shifted.

Now that he had a gun, he developed a godlike complex. That feeling of knowing he could do what he wanted, to whoever he wanted, and nobody could stop him if he had the drop.

Even the most powerful men in the world couldn't walk away from a bullet to the head like it never happened.

And with that altered ego came a new fearlessness, one that started the music to his dance with the devil.

After stealing the car and breaking into the abandoned house, he decided to add both to his arsenal. One gave him mobility in the streets. The other gave him access to people's property. Not to mention, it gave him more space to stash loot, if it was worth holding onto.

Now, all he needed was a fence. Somebody to act as middleman for the stolen goods. Turn them into cash for him. That way, he wouldn't have to get caught red-handed trying to flip them himself.

But when you start dancing with the devil…

You better make sure *you're* the one who stops the music.

CHAPTER 4

"Can you believe this old ass nigga bro talkin' 'bout 'take 'em on a rough ride then bring 'em to me'?" Mike said to Tony, still heated after their call with Booker. "Who the fuck that old Jerry Rice-lookin' ass nigga think he is? Don Corleone or some damn body?"

Carrying on with his usual insubordination, Mike kept ranting. "He lucky I ain't Fleewell. I woulda took him for everything, erased that camera footage, and smoked his bitch ass *str8 up*."

Tony just started laughing like always, letting his boy vent. He knew Mike had a bit of an authority problem, that's why they'd always been fifty-fifty partners.

Switching gears, but still on topic, Tony said, "As a matter of fact, call that nigga Fleewell on that burner phone we gave him. We need to go grab that *before* he do somethin' stupid."

He was talking about the cheap dollar-store flip phone they'd given Fleewell just to stay in contact after the sting they'd staged to get that firearm from Booker. That gun was supposed to play a vital role in taking him out and solidifying their rise to the top.

Mike did as told, dialed the number, but no luck. Couldn't reach the basehead.

Paranoia started creeping in, but Tony tried to keep it cool. "Maybe the phone died," he suggested. "You know how much that fool be on the go, probably ain't had time to stop and charge it."

Tired of sitting around waiting for him to show up at the trap like they agreed, they decided to be proactive. They hopped in the car and started hitting all the spots he was known to frequent. They had to catch up with him before the streets, or worse, *Booker*, did.

They knew what was at stake and couldn't afford for Booker to get suspicious too soon. Not with everything that was really going on behind the scenes…

Booker, now feeling vulnerable in this elite game of chess, knew exactly what his ultimate tool was, *money*. And he used it very well to gain an advantage over any given threat.

Sitting at the desk in his pawn shop office, he started digging through drawers, searching for his address book, the one with all his most important contacts. There was a specific number he had in mind.

The more he went over that surveillance footage of Fleewell robbing him, the more it felt *too* calculated. Fleewell didn't even look up when Booker slid the gun under the counter yet went straight to it like he knew exactly where it would be.

And that kind of move? That instinct? That only came from somebody who'd been around him *a lot* more than Fleewell ever had.

It was time to play some defense.

After flipping through a bunch of disorganized papers, he finally found the number he was looking for and quickly dialed it.

First ring, someone picked up.

"Oliver's Private Investigations Office. How may I help you?" a deep, monotone voice came through.

Booker, not sure how else to confirm his suspicions, had called the one man he knew could dig deep *without* alerting anybody that he was even onto them, Oliver Maxwell. An ex-FBI analyst turned private investigator, Oliver had helped Booker in the past, like the time he caught his wife cheating with her personal trainer. Left her penniless in the divorce, even though Booker had *also* been unfaithful first.

This was chess. Not checkers.

"Yeah, can I speak to Oliver? Tell 'em this Booker," he said.

He got placed on hold as the assistant patched him through.

Oliver came on the line with that smooth, Keith Sweat-type voice Booker would recognize anywhere.

"Long time no speak, my friend. How's it going? Not any more unknown polygamy for me to deal with, I hope?" Oliver joked, referring to their last situation.

"Nah, man. Not this time. One prison bid was enough for me," Booker said, chuckling lightly. "I'm still a bachelor now, bro. But I *do* got bigger problems on my hands. I could use your services."

He leaned forward in his chair.

"So why don't chu stop by when it's convenient for you? I'll make it worth your while. You know the money's always good. Then I'll bring you up to speed on my little situation. I don't trust these phone lines no more, *especially* after all that shit you showed me last time."

Oliver accepted. Said he'd swing by sometime tomorrow after finishing up with another client. Then they hung up.

Booker leaned back in his chair, feeling good about the next move he'd already set in motion. He checked his Rolex and started to wonder what was taking Tony and Mike so long to bring him Fleewell.

Negatively assuming the worst, he figured they were probably somewhere trying to get their stories straight.

Deep in thought, Booker dozed off.

Meanwhile, Tony and Mike were driving around the city like a game of *Pac-Man*, hitting every corner of Fleewell's known hangouts, and still no luck.

That's when they finally made contact with one of his smoker buddies.

The man told them exactly where to find Fleewell: the County Jail.

The news hit hard.

Fleewell had been arrested on a couple unrelated home invasion charges, plus a flight to avoid arrest. He was now

41

sitting in the county, and it threw a whole new set of obstacles in their path.

Time to strategize. Next move had to be the *best* move.

First, they needed to find out what his exact charges were. If he hadn't been caught with anything *extra*, they still had a chance.

Then, they needed to contact him ASAP and figure out what the hell happened to the *gun*.

Wasting no time, Tony and Mike headed straight downtown to the County Jail while there was still daylight. After going through a quick screening process, they gained entry and provided the credentials needed to visit Fleewell via video monitor.

As they entered the visitation area, they saw other people sitting at booths, talking to loved ones through computer screens. Phones were attached to the sides, cameras locked in, and every inmate on the other side wore orange jumpsuits and the same detached expression.

Tony and Mike sat at their assigned booth, picked up the receiver, and the feed came to life.

Now they were face-to-face with the man of the hour: Fleewell Jones.

"Wassup, nigga? What the fuck happened, man? I thought we had a deal!" Tony was first to speak, clearly upset. Things were *not* going according to plan, but he tried to keep his voice down.

"Man, Larry O and 'em turned me on to a suite in the neighborhood not far from y'all spot, so I punched the clock," Fleewell said, like it was just another day.

"Larry O" was the same smoker buddy who'd told them where to find him. And a "suite" in Fleewell language meant a home invasion, referencing the in-and-out nature of the job like it was a hotel.

Tony damn near lost it.

"I don't give a fuck 'bout none of that extra shit! You should've just stuck to the plan, dude, *damn*! And I told you we was gon' take care of you, didn't I? And I ain't never lied to you. Now look at chu!"

He was way more emotional than he wanted to be, but this whole thing was starting to fall apart right in front of them.

Fleewell just put his head down in submission, knowing he'd messed up. Then he looked back up and said what Tony and Mike came to hear, but it was also the last thing they wanted to hear.

"I know I fucked up y'all trust in me on this one, man. But if y'all bond me out, I'll take y'all straight to where I threw the loot."

It was Mike who jumped in, hot as a teakettle.

"Nigga, you did what?!"

Fleewell looked for some compassion in his eyes, but there was none.

43

"Look man, I couldn't get caught up with no piece. I'm already a big-time felon, big dawg. And they already talkin' 'bout enhancin' these charges and hittin' me with the bitch on this if my prints on anything in that suite they swept."

The bitch, meaning habitual criminal, carried a minimum of ten years, day for day. They wouldn't recommend it in his case, since being labeled a career criminal after several felonious convictions meant he ran the risk of spending the rest of his natural life in prison if convicted again.

Mike, not wanting to expose his hand too early, knew Fleewell had leverage right now. He tried to reason with him, hoping to work out some kind of deal.

"How 'bout this, you tell us where to find what we lookin' for, and if everything is everything, I'll have you outta here by tomorrow. Word is bond."

Fleewell, confident they'd find exactly what they were looking for and that they'd keep their word, agreed. He figured there wasn't a soul in sight that saw him toss the loot. The cops had been too far and too lazy to trace every step of the hour-long chase before they caught him. So, he gave up the exact spot, but only after they agreed that whatever else they found, they'd hold for him until he got out.

Coming from the county and headed toward the location Fleewell gave them, Tony and Mike made a quick stop at Tony's sister's house to drop off some grocery money for the kids. Tony always prided himself on being a provider, especially for family.

Approaching the car to grab the money was his favorite niece, Patrese Walker, his sister's oldest. She was fifteen, in high school, but looking more like twenty-five the way she was filling out. She had the appearance of an Instagram model.

"Wassup, Uncle T? My mama said I'm 'posed to come grab somethin' from you," she said, way too much attitude in her voice.

"Yeah, I gotchu right here, Pat. And tell yo bighead mama I said next time, some personal gratitude gon' be required with her bougie ass. Now getcho lil fast ass back in the house and put some more clothes on."

Coming outside with her bottom half barely covered by some booty shorts, she just shook her head and smiled, then thanked her uncle and did as she was told.

A short while later, they pulled up to the exact location Fleewell had given them to find the stash. Mike hopped out to check behind the big green dumpster, in the exact spot described.

Frustration built quickly when it wasn't there.

He searched all around, underneath, in between, through every stinking trash bag in the area, but didn't find a single thing Fleewell said would be there.

Coming back to the car empty-handed had both Tony and Mike heated. They decided to make a few calls to people they knew in the county, contacts they kept on standby for situations just like this.

After a long conversation with some of their hitters inside, going over what needed to be done to tie up a couple loose ends, they set a new plan in motion. One that hadn't been part of the original.

They hung up and headed straight to the pawn shop to give Booker the bad news and hopefully walk out alive.

Another sit-down with the devil, and they were in a position neither one of them could've planned for…

Booker woke up to his phone ringing nonstop. He hadn't realized he'd been asleep for hours. Glancing at the caller ID, he quickly answered, trying to sound as smooth and player as possible.

"Hey baby, I just was over here thinkin' 'bout cho fine ass. How you doin' today, beautiful?" he said, standing up out the chair for a quick stretch, still stiff from his catnap.

The young lady on the other end replied, "Good. And when am I gon' be able to see you again? My mom goin' outta town this weekend for a couple days, and I can have my best friend come watch my siblings for me while I'm gone. You can have me all to yoself."

The girl was so young, she had to be real cautious and always maneuvering around family and friends just to keep their relationship afloat. Booker gave her financial security and pleasure, and he had plenty of experience.

"I don't know if that's a good idea, Pat. I got a lot goin' on right now. I'm needin' to pay more attention to," Booker started, talking down to her like he didn't have time for their secret situation.

That pissed Patrese off.

She went to her go-to move that always got him to do exactly what she wanted.

"Oh, so you ain't got no time for me now? Is that what you sayin'? Always thinkin' you entertainin' other young bitches," she snapped, knowing his taste too well. "And how much time you think you gon' have when my mama and my uncle find out, huh?"

Now she had Booker by the balls.

He quickly started trying to de-escalate, seeing where this was headed.

"Nah, nah, nah, it ain't nothin' like that. I'ma be to see you soon. You know I can't stay away from you for long. It's just some funny business goin' on in my crew with these cats in the streets I deal with. I need to get to the bottom of it first, that's all. Then I come getchu and we can go do anything you want."

Booker laid it on thick, soothing and slick.

Giving in to his charisma, she replied, "You know what I wanna do, Daddy… Okay then, I guess I'll call you in a couple days and let you handle yo business, my love. Be careful."

They said their goodbyes, and he hung up, cursing himself out for falling into yet another situation bound to spin out of control. But for now, he had to roll with the punches, feeling like he still had everything and everybody under control.

Then, as if he breathed them into existence, Tony and Mike came walking up the sidewalk, entering the pawn shop through the front door just as Booker leaned over to check the camera monitors.

47

"Bossman, where you at?" Tony called out, walking in first with Mike right behind.

"I'm in my office. Come on back, fellas," Booker answered, already seated behind his desk. Two chairs sat on the other side as they stepped in.

"Please, have a seat. I've been waitin' on y'all for hours. Give me some news I can use," he said, still patronizing. "And please tell me that nigga outside in the Benz trunk."

Tony took a deep breath and locked eyes with him.

"That's actually what we came here to talk to you about, Boss. See, we did what you asked, searched the city for that nigga Flee. Then we came across a buddy of his who told us he got arrested for a home invasion and was in the county, facin' serious time.

"So, then we go down there to bond him out just to grab him for you… and muthafuckas in the county told us… he hung himself."

You could almost see the smoke coming out of Booker's nose and ears, like an animated cartoon.

He was *furious* with these latest developments.

Unable to hold his composure anymore, Booker snapped.

"The fuck you mean that nigga hung hisself?! Ain't no way. So, you tellin' me that my gun is just out in the elements somewhere?! Man, go round up every fuckin' swerve that done seen him in the last 24 hours and find out where he went! I don't care how long it takes either, or don't be expectin' no re-up this week 'til y'all find it!"

The gun was too important to him. It held secrets of its own.

Booker couldn't afford to let it surface on his watch. He'd committed his first homicide with that pistol, and a few more after, that paved the way for him to become one of the top dogs today. He never let it get far from his reach. Kept it as a status symbol ever since the work he put in with it back in the '80s.

It had originally belonged to his grandfather, who passed it down to him. And since Booker didn't even have so much as a speeding ticket on his record, completely off the radar, he'd never come under suspicion for any of it. Never even thought to get rid of the gun.

Especially since nobody he chose to deal with even knew his real name.

But now, with that piece missing, he could feel the tides turning. Stuck between a rock and a hard place, he couldn't even report it stolen because of the *damaging* timeline that gun held, if it ended up in police custody.

Calming down just enough, but still fuming, he said to Tony and Mike:

"Now get the fuck out my office…"

Fleewell paced around in his cell, hoping everything was going according to plan. But the longer he sat there, the more nervous he got.

Even with a rap sheet as long as the Declaration of Independence, Fleewell *hated* jail. Could never get used to doing time, walking around in those uncomfortable-ass flip flops, in raggedy clothes, surrounded by energy that made the whole place feel wrong.

He looked around his unit for the first time, not recognizing anybody, nobody he'd victimized on one of his crack binges, or owed for smoking up their stash.

He took that as a sign of relief. Relaxed a little, knowing he didn't have any immediate enemies around him that posed a threat.

Not having shaved or showered in weeks, he decided to clean himself up before the evening meal. Figured by the time he got himself together and put something on his stomach, the day would be over, and Tony and Mike would be there to get him out in the morning, like they promised.

With no money on his inmate account, he borrowed some hygiene items from staff. Then headed into the shower area, which was off camera, and started to clean up.

It felt like a scary movie.

All the lights went out for a quick second just as he stepped into an available stall. He turned on the water, started washing himself, completely unaware of what was about to go down.

Watching Fleewell ever since he entered the unit was a six-foot-four, 280-pound killer named Tex. He was down for a double homicide, with only one witness against him, and had been questioned in multiple other states for more.

Tex was a certified hitman.

And after being promised a hefty payout by a crooked staff member he compromised, Tex had been moved to this unit just to get the job done. He had one goal in mind, and it was time to earn his attorney's fees. He could practically feel his freedom closing in.

As soon as the power glitched, Tex entered the shower area right behind Fleewell. Came up on him from the back and strangled him to death.

The fragile smoker never stood a chance.

By the time he realized he wasn't alone in that stall, it was too late.

Tex, experienced with this type of kill, strung the same cord he used to strangle Fleewell up through the vent above the shower. Made it look like a suicide. Then walked out the same way he came in, cool, quiet, calm.

As far as anyone else knew...

It never even happened.

The guard on shift had already been paid off.

The quick power outage glitched the cameras just long enough for Tex and Fleewell to enter the showers unseen.

Erased. Just like Fleewell's existence.

Tony and Mike exited Booker's establishment. Once they got back to the car, they took a moment to talk and vent their frustrations.

They got all that off their chest quick, then Tony checked his messages to make sure everything had gone according to plan.

Once he got the confirmations, he had Mike transfer the funds into anonymous accounts prearranged for everyone involved in the conspiracy.

After that, they decided to hit the strip club. It was their usual spot.

Time to blow off some steam and clear their minds from the day that just refused to go right.

They made a vow: come tomorrow, they'd have a more strategic plan. One that'd put them ahead of the game.

Meanwhile, across town…

Patrese Walker pretended like she was going to sleep, waiting for her mother to come check on her before heading out for the graveyard shift.

The second she heard her mama's car pull out the driveway, she jumped up and called one of her flings to come stay the night.

Hot and horny, anticipating his arrival, she called up her best friend Chealsey to gossip about school, and all the boys they were into.

Picking up the house phone, she reached Chealsey after a few rings.

"Hey girl, what'chu doin'?" Patrese said into the receiver, laying flat on her stomach in bed, kicking her legs in the air like she was swimming.

"Nothin', just got off the phone with Kia's crazy ass. Wyd?" Chealsey replied, talking about their mutual friend.

"Layin' in my bed waitin' on Keith to come put this fire out for tonight. You know my mama workin' all night now at the hospital. But what she was talkin' 'bout?" Patrese asked, excited.

"Girl, you gon' fuck around and catch somethin' you keep it up," Chealsey shot back. "And that silly bitch talkin' 'bout she want Miles to be her baby daddy."

"Probably 'cause she think he goin' to the league," Patrese said, annoyed. "That bitch ain't slick. But I been wantin' me a thug like Tay, girl, I ain't gon' lie."

"But anyways, I gotta go, girl. I think that's Keith outside now," Patrese said, cutting the convo short.

The girls said their goodbyes.

CHAPTER 5

As days turned to weeks, and weeks into months, some time passed, and football season finally arrived.

Miteous had his head on straight for the most part, not avoiding Tay Vaughn entirely, but definitely steering clear of the aftermath he *knew* was coming his way, especially with all the dust he'd been hearing Tay was kicking up during his extracurricular activity.

Meanwhile, Miteous was working hard at practice every day. He poured all his time and energy into making an enthusiastic effort to impress his coaches with his speed, agility, and sheer will during every skills drill and man-on-man competition he was inserted into. He wanted to make sure he earned his playing time.

More importantly, he wanted all eyes on him come Friday night, under the lights, when reputations were on the line and spectators watched every time he touched the ball. That's when he could put on a full display of exactly what he could do, and exactly how much better he was than everyone else.

Hopefully, that would secure a brighter future for him and his family.

This became his routine week to week during the season. Occasionally, he'd step out on the weekends for some fun. But then it was right back to grinding.

Never, not once, did he wholeheartedly take the time out to give God the glory for the gifts and talents He'd bestowed upon him. But Miteous was always the first one on the field and the last one off. Just like dinnertime at home, his mom would cook his favorite meal, and he'd always thank her afterward.

She had always taught him that hard work would get him where he wanted to go. Consistency would keep him there. And gratitude? That would make it all multiply. He stuck to that religiously.

However, what he never fully realized was: you are the company you keep.

Because birds of a feather flock together.

Miteous kept his nose clean by staying out of trouble. He made good grades and attended all his classes. He didn't really have time for anything else, trying to maintain this balanced lifestyle so he could chase his dreams uninterrupted.

But he did leave his mind, and his nose, open to one thing.

One thing that would eventually tip the scale and offset the balance.

Girls.

Which were supposed to be the glory of man... but since the beginning of time had often contributed to being the exact opposite once they entered the picture.

There comes a time in every young man's life, and everybody's life, for that matter, when they realize how short this existence really is. And that maybe it ain't meant to be spent alone.

That's when the hunt begins.

Growing up in a two-parent household, love was always in the air, so nobody necessarily had to "have the talk" with Miteous. He was always observant. A good listener when he wanted to be, especially when grown folks were around.

He knew that whenever the adults got together, explicit content was always gonna get aired out by everybody who knew everybody else's business.

And growing up in a family that enjoyed annual get-togethers and weekend festivities, he was never more than an earshot away from the latest gossip and drama, about one relative or another's adulterous affairs or scandals. Like a living, breathing Lifetime newsfeed.

So, he became conscious early on about the game men and women have been running on each other since forever. He even heard stories from his elders that said that was how a lot of his people made it out of slavery back in the day.

He stored all that information in his mental files for later.

And it came in handy the day he finally decided to make good use of the playerism he'd inherited, when fate lined up the perfect opportunity.

It was a sunny Saturday afternoon.

He'd had a long week of practice in preparation for his first game, and homework every night from his teachers who kept challenging him in his advanced classes. Now all Miteous needed was some nice, wholesome fun and some fresh outdoors to blow off steam.

So, he decided to go to the local park to play some pickup basketball with the fellas.

Even though he wasn't the best basketball player, he always jumped at the chance to show off his athleticism in any physical sport.

He let his mama know where he was headed, and a little while later arrived at the park. Coming within one hundred yards of it, he could already hear the screams and shouts of kids, teens, and young adults all having a good time, fully engaged in their own activities.

He knew it was packed. And instantly got excited too, ready to see who all showed up.

When Miteous finally made it to the blacktop, he looked around and spotted several familiar faces. It felt like everybody from a 20-mile radius had decided to come to the park that day.

And who could blame them? The weather was perfect, not too hot, not too cold. If it hadn't been so windy, it might've been the best day of the year so far.

He took in the whole scene, vibing off the energy in the air. Dozens of people, laughing, playing, running around. It was all so harmonious. It put him in a sort of daydream state, like he wasn't even there anymore.

Then, thud.

A bump on the back of his heel brought him back to reality. Startled but not scared, he instinctively turned around with his guard up, ready to take on the heavyweight champ… only to see a child's ball had rolled up and hit his leg.

It had come from somewhere off in the distance.

He bent down and picked it up, and that's when he saw *her*.

A young woman jogging over in his direction. And when he turned to get a better look at her face, he was frustrated that the sun was behind her, lighting her up from behind and temporarily blinding him.

But what he *did* notice right away…

Some healthy double D breasts on a five-foot-five frame, light-skinned, with childbearing hips popping out from her skin-tight spandex. She was confidently showing off her figure, and she had his *full and undivided* attention.

She was *so* fine.

"Sorry about that! I was over there tryin' to teach my nephew how to throw and catch the ball. Must've gotten away from 'em. Some teacher I am," the girl said, laughing innocently as she approached.

Still standing in front of the sun, Miteous had to raise a hand over his eyes like a soldier's salute just to see her face.

And when he finally did?

His gut filled with butterflies. It felt like fate had lined this up for him.

He wasn't about to hold back.

"Veronica? Veronica Taylor, is that you? Damn, it's been a minute! I hardly even recognized you after all these years."

She took a second to study his face. Familiarity sparked as she searched her mental database.

"Miteous Reese's?" she said hesitantly, more like a question than an answer.

That was all he needed.

It gave Miteous the momentum, and the energy, to work up the courage to make his first move. He wasn't about to let her get away from him again.

All he could think about now was staying engaged with her while he had the opportunity.

Now that the familiarity was there, he just needed to add some comfortability, and he'd be all the way in.

He attempted to make more conversation, doing what came naturally to his mind. He remembered all the game he'd soaked up over the years. He knew women were always signaling their wants, needs, likes, and dislikes, it's just that most men were too selfish or too distracted to notice.

But not Miteous.

And not this time.

He flashed a charming smile at her, then tossed the ball back.

She caught it and smiled right back.

"Seem like they workin' pretty good to me now… Where lil' man at so I can see if it run in the family? Unless I ain't invited to come and play with y'all," Miteous said charismatically.

Veronica pondered it for a quick second before finally giving in, going against any adverse thoughts she may've had prior. She gave him a once-over that said she usually didn't just invite strangers around her nephew, especially ones she didn't plan on having around long.

But she quickly became comfortable with Miteous again, after all this time, and just went with the flow. She brought him over to the area where they'd been playing catch.

There, he met her nephew, looked to be about five years old. Then Miteous stepped in for her and started playing with him, going back and forth, throwing and receiving the ball. The kid had endless energy and a surprisingly decent throwing arm for his age. His name was Garrison.

As they played, Miteous kept talking to Veronica, learning more and more about her and who she'd become over the last decade since they'd last seen each other. The more he found out, the more intrigued he became. And the more intrigued he got, the more aggressive his pursuit.

The less she resisted over time, the further she allowed things to escalate between them.

The deeper their connection became.

Running a football and getting away with felonies wasn't the only thing Miteous was good at anymore.

So was seducing women...

Tay Vaughn couldn't wait for school to let out. Even if he was only going half the time nowadays, still felt like he had better things to do with his time than learn shit he wouldn't even need in the streets.

And lately, he'd been committed to the streets like it was his community service.

It wasn't a soul in sight to dispute the fact that Tay had the streets written all over him now.

Indulging hopelessly into crime like he was born for it.

And it didn't take a rocket scientist to see that it'd been weighing on him, too.

He was in desperate need of love and affection. Even thugs got feelings.

But what he *really* needed was some relief, intimate companionship.

Someone he could genuinely confide in, even if only for a moment.

It was time for Tay to turn down his gangster some and turn up his player more.

Because even though he was a knucklehead, he knew a man without women?

That ain't how evolution worked.

That's when Tay Vaughn Kelly's hunt began.

It'd been a few weeks since Tay got to hang out with Miteous like they usually did.

He'd seen him around and they'd speak, but didn't really think anything of it.

He'd known Miteous for so long, knew how serious he was about trying to make it in sports, especially football. And he knew this time of year, Miteous got real distant from everybody and everything that could be a distraction. He locked in.

Even though Tay probably never told him out loud, he respected that. Admired it, even.

Miteous wasn't just gifted, he was a hard worker.

That motivated Tay to be better at *his* craft, too.

Even if it came with consequences.

Not being able to consult with his right-hand man like usual had Tay feeling withdrawn.

The streets had never allowed anyone else to get that close to him before.

Nobody else really understood or related to his struggle.

That created a void in Tay, one he was long overdue to fill.

Growing up how he did, basically having to look after himself his whole life, Tay didn't really know what a healthy relationship looked like. Not outside of movie scripts and TV.

Let alone how to build one for himself.

Especially not with all the trust issues he had from childhood trauma.

But he *definitely* knew what sex was.

Just not how good it actually felt, yet.

He'd never experienced it for himself.

All that changed one afternoon after school, with someone he least expected.

Someone who opened up his mind to a whole new feeling…

One he couldn't help but start chasing afterward.

Euphoria.

After school let out, Tay navigated his way through the crowded frenzy, over a thousand people going their own separate ways like at an airport and headed straight to Granny's house.

Not that the house belonged to his *actual* grandmother or anything.

It was a code name he and Miteous came up with for the abandoned property he used to stash stolen loot, hang out, or crash when he had nowhere else to go.

He didn't like going to his mama's house unless he had to, too many people coming in and out at all hours of the night. Too much unwanted company.

He entered through the back like always and went straight to his stash, just to make sure everything was where he left it. Not that he had any reason to worry, nobody even knew about it.

But in his line of work, you could never be too sure.

There ain't no honor among thieves.

After putting his mind at ease, Tay found a spot in the corner of the room to post up, kick back, and think. He ran through a couple plans he'd been cooking up, reviewing them more thoroughly now that he didn't have distractions throwing off his train of thought.

He knew for a fact that what he was doing to survive wouldn't last forever.

He'd seen it with his own eyes.

People who tried to make it in the same game he was playing and fell by the wayside.

So, whatever he decided to do next, it had to be worth his time.

He only had one life.

But that didn't stop him from playing it the only way he knew how.

He had no intention of leaving the game behind.

He just wanted to come up with a better strategy, to get more out of it, with less work and less risk.

Running some imaginary numbers in his head, Tay totaled up what he had and where he wanted to be. He knew he had a lot of work to do.

At the top of his priority list?

Finding a fence, someone to move stolen goods through buyers for him, so he could stay anonymous and flip it to quick cash.

And finding a plug, someone with access to drugs he could buy in bulk and sell for more.

He knew exactly who could point him in the right direction.

Hopefully to both.

But for sure, the drugs.

Before Tay left Granny's house, he grabbed his money and his gun.

Then left the same way he came in, leaving behind only the jewelry and other items he planned to move later.

He'd stolen several cars since his first one but never drove them longer than 72 hours.

Never parked them near anywhere he planned to be for more than an hour, either. Most of the time, he'd just leave them on busy streets or in random lots.

He always kept them in different areas close to where he'd be for the moment, just in case they got discovered or towed. That way, nobody could say they saw him get in or out.

Because of this system, he always stuck to walking a short distance to and from.

And it worked.

Sure enough, around the corner, he found one that hadn't been touched since last week.

He hopped in and headed toward his mom's best friend's house, Ms. Ebony.

He parked a few blocks away to avoid nosy neighbors making connections between him and the car. That little detail played a big role in why he'd never been caught.

That, and the fact he always wiped down *everything* he touched during a crime, just like his mama taught him since he was a kid.

Her number one rule?

"You don't get caught."

So extra precautions? That was just standard procedure.

Tay walked the rest of the way to Ms. Ebony's place and made it to her duplex.

Almost knocked on the wrong door, been a while since he came over by himself, not accompanied by his mother.

But desperate times called for desperate measures.

Furthermore, considering the fact that Ms. Ebony and his mom had been doing dirt and drugs together since before he was even thought of, she made the perfect candidate to have the connections he needed to advance his career in the underworld.

Knocking lightly on her door, Tay stood there and waited patiently, hoping she was home now. As he stood there, he started thinking about his next move if this one didn't go accordingly. Not that he was a pessimist or anything, but he was a strong believer that when you plan, you always gotta plan for the plan not going according to plan as well.

Then, interrupting his thoughts, Ms. Ebony came to the door, hair all over the place, nothing but a bathrobe on, looking like she'd just woken up. She was about five-foot-three, jet-black hair, dark-skinned, with nice big breasts that sagged a little. Flat stomach from never having kids, but wide, childbearing hips that held up a heart-shaped ass.

If it hadn't been for all the drug abuse, and God only knew what else, it looked like she might've had real potential back in her prime. But she was still fine for a middle-aged smoker.

Greeting Tay after opening her door, she recognized him immediately and said,

"Hey baby, what chu doin' over here? Did I leave somethin' over yo mom's again when I came by earlier?"

Completely surprised by his visit.

"Nah, Ms. Ebony, I came by on my own. I was hopin' I could holler atchu for a second bout some shit real quick if you got a minute. I hope I ain't catch you at a bad time, did I?" Tay replied, referencing her raggedy appearance all melodramatic.

Ms. Ebony, being as seasoned as she was, already knew what this visit was about. She couldn't help but try and take advantage of the situation, knowing Tay was always adamant about advancing his quality of life through the streets. Especially having known his mother since before he was born and knowing that's all she taught him since he could steal for her.

She knew this day was coming.

And not wanting to feel like a predator by admitting it, she'd kind of been waiting on it too.

"Please, come on in. And boy, I done told you a thousand times to just call me *Ebony*, you grown now. But what chu got on yo mind that's makin' yo face so long? You too blessed to be stressed now," Ebony said with a mischievous smile, holding the door open with her arm stretched so he could see her breasts if he looked hard enough on his way in.

Then she closed the door behind them and walked straight past the living room to her bedroom, silently hoping he'd follow right behind her like he did, so it wouldn't make things awkward.

Shortly after entering Ebony's house, Tay noticed a sensational fragrance in the air, stimulating and reassuring. But not wanting to intrude, he never said anything about it. Just kept following her until she found somewhere comfortable enough to finish their conversation.

Still following her lead, Tay said,

"Awh okay den. If I'm blessed, I hate to see what bein' cursed feel like, I ain't got a pot to piss in or a window to throw it out of. But I could use yo help with a couple things."

They'd reached her room, and he noticed a candle lit, that's where the lovely aroma came from. He always liked when a woman kept her house clean and smelling good.

"Talk to me then. You know I always got yo back," Ebony replied with her own agenda in mind. Sitting down on the edge of her bed, she picked her leg up slowly, crossing one over the other all ladylike, then patted the spot next to her, signaling him to have a seat.

Then she grabbed a blunt from her ashtray, already rolled on her nightstand, sparked it up and took a long drag.

Tay was so focused on presenting his proposition, he didn't even notice her whole vibe had shifted. Or the sexual signals she'd been giving him through her body language since they got back there. He just kept pushing forward with what was on his mind.

"Well, I know you know I know bout you and my moms gettin' high and everything like that. So, I was just wonderin' if you could introduce me to yo connect so I could cop from em. And y'all just deal with me. But just don't let her know it's me then she gon' think somebody owe her ass somethin', and I ain't never gon' be able to make no money.

"And I wanted to know if you knew anybody that could fence some high-quality jewels. Cause one of my guys tryna get rid of some shit."

Not wanting to expose his whole hand too quickly, he was more interested in finding out what *she* had to offer because *his* deck really held all the cards.

Passing Tay the blunt, then exhaling, Ebony started nodding her head in agreement before she spoke.

"That don't sound like a bad idea, Tay. I think I might can hook that up for you… if yo money right. And you willin' to bless yo girl by lookin' out, I gotchu.

"But I ain't really got no one that come to mind about the other thing. But I'll ask around and letchu know if I do hear somethin'."

That made Tay flash his little charismatic smile, excited. He pulled out a nice-sized bankroll of hundreds and waved it in front of her.

"Aww I'ma have the bread, and I'ma look out for you, don't even trip off that," he said arrogantly, now that everything seemed to be going exactly how he planned.

Seeing the money, and the type of man TayVaughn was becoming, had Ebony turned all the way on. She smiled back at him seductively and said,

"I know that's right… Look atchu out here makin' moves."

Getting the blunt back from him, she took another long drag before blowing smoke out her nose and mouth. She started getting hot all over. Then she took control of the narrative.

"Now let me ask *you* somethin', young man," Ebony said, putting the blunt out in her ashtray.

Tay just looked at her suspiciously, hoping she wasn't about to ask for no money, he hated being the bearer of bad news. He waited to see what she had to say first and replied,

"Wassup wit it?" nodding at her like he was greeting her in passing.

Ebony could be real blunt at times, being an older woman, she just said whatever she felt. Tay liked that about her. He always saw weakness in people who sugarcoated everything instead of keepin' it one hundred. He could relate, being a straight shooter himself.

"You seein' anybody these days? Not that it's any of my business or nothin', but I know how stressful of a lifestyle it is, and I can see it weighin' on you," she said, not trying to be rude.

Tay thought about it for a second, then let out a deep breath.

"I ain't really got no time to think about shit else out here tryna make it happen for myself, you know. But I *know* I could use a woman's touch right about now."

Without much confidence.

Ebony took that as her cue to release all the sexual tension he didn't even know he had. She started massaging his shoulders, rubbing her hands down his chest, then replied,

"How about mine?"

Like a porn star.

Leaning into him slowly, she kissed and caressed his neck, groping his inner thigh where she could feel his manhood growing, inch by inch. And instantly, she got wet just anticipating the full length.

Tay got so aroused he couldn't even find his voice to respond after she got started.

He just let Ebony take complete control of the situation.

She began to aggressively mount him, peeling off another piece of his clothing with every move. All Tay could do was make her job easier by complying with every instruction.

He met every demand.

From that point on, he was in foreign territory.

No longer a virgin anymore.

Not only was he able to make the connections he needed to advance his agenda in the streets...

But he also got the release he needed as well.

Even better, it was all in the same place.

And Tay *knew* this wasn't gonna be the last time either.

Especially after how good he made her feel the first go-round.

Gave him a huge boost in confidence after satisfying an older woman who had definitely been around the block. He couldn't wait to brag to Miteous when he got the chance, knowing he had one up on him now.

And now that he knew what he was doing?

He couldn't wait to start doing it with all the girls his own age who were curious about the experience with him.

What Tay didn't know though...

Was that they were already waiting on him.

Especially with his reputation as a bad boy.

And what good girl didn't already have her eyes dead set on one of *those*…

CHAPTER 6

"No man lives unto himself, for every living thing is bound by cords to every other thing."

Elihu's lesson: *The Unity of Life.* Because we are all connected.

It seemed like the perfect storm, with everything going right at the time for Miteous and TayVaughn, that could've gone completely wrong. Hitting licks, then flying straight down their own respected paths.

Miteous was thriving in football, entertaining new love interests, and a few other women he just couldn't turn down. After word spread through the grapevine that he was good in bed, everyone who'd heard it wanted a piece. He couldn't resist confirming the rumors himself, especially with the football fans.

Occasionally, he'd step out with Tay if Tay had a couple girls and needed backup. But only after Miteous was assured she knew who he was and what he was on, guaranteeing Tay he was gonna get laid.

TayVaughn, meanwhile, had been spending more time with Ebony, and through her, met her connect. That turned him into one of Alibi Mac's main corner boys. It solidified a relationship that worked out well for both of them, allowing the local hype to be served by Tay so Alibi wouldn't have to deal with lowlifes and could just sit back and collect the money.

Even though Tay wasn't getting rich off it, it was still a consistent income. And that alone kept him from risking his freedom with all the stealing that brought on way more heat. He thrived to survive. But this whole little ghetto utopia they'd created for themselves came to a sudden halt... once both their networks expanded, and their paths started colliding.

One day after football practice, Miteous was getting dressed in the locker room after a shower, thinking about a few plans he had in mind for the weekend. He'd heard about this senior girl's party, a girl he'd already had relations with, and figured it'd be a good place to scout for some new tail.

That's when he accidentally overheard a conversation between a couple guys from the team that he shouldn't have... but later was glad he did.

"Ay bro, remember I was tellin' you 'bout my uncle that owns that pawn shop downtown?" Sammy D said.

He was leading the state in tackles and had been made team leader on defense. He was talking to one of his defensive linemen named Leon, someone he was real close with, who was always one of the last ones to leave.

"Yeah, I 'member foo. You only bring that shit up all the time, how much bread the nigga got and all dat. But what about him?" Leon replied, uninterested, just a little too loud while packing all his gear into an already crammed locker.

He didn't know Miteous was standing off to the side, a couple locker rows back in the shadows, heading out the locker room until he heard that last part and stopped in his tracks, just out of curiosity.

"Well, I only go by there every so often, but when I stopped by the last time, he told me if I knew anybody tryna get rid of some nice shit, to let him know. So let me know if you hear anything. And I gotchu, seein' as how you was tellin' me 'bout all them scandals yo moms got goin' on at the club, always gettin' niggas for they shit, let her know you know where she can unload it and get cashed out, no questions asked. That's all I'm sayin'," Sammy D said, respectful as possible. He was trying to create an opportunity for himself instead of a conflict he knew he couldn't resolve on his own.

Miteous had talked with the six-foot-five, three-hundred-pound lineman before about how much he hated what his mom did for a living, even if it did put clothes on his back.

"Aight, that's what's up bro. That's good lookin' out, I'll letchu know. But let's be out though," Big Leon replied, standing up and towering over Sammy D as they embraced in a handshake before heading toward the exit, last ones to leave the locker room.

The next day at school, Miteous couldn't wait to tell TayVaughn what he'd heard so they could put their heads together and capitalize off this business opportunity themselves.

Searching all around school for him, he finally found Tay hugged up in a back hallway with some girl Miteous had never met before. He hesitated for a second, not wanting to interrupt Tay's groove, so he walked up quietly behind him and nudged him urgently, signaling with his head that he needed to talk in private immediately.

76

For a second, Tay knew something was up. Miteous didn't normally act like this. So, he smoothly excused himself from the convo he was having with the girl he'd just started vibing with, who had unexpectedly caught his attention.

Her name was Patrese Walker.

Tay had just found that out.

He stepped away just far enough that their conversation couldn't be overheard. Miteous's whole facial expression changed into one of excitement as soon as it was just the two of them.

"Ay bro, you can't tell me I don't be at the right places at the right time," Miteous said, then brought Tay up to speed on everything he'd overheard yesterday.

"So basically, we can just go down there, drop ol' boy name, and show 'em what we got, right?" Miteous said, emphasis heavy on the last part. More of a question than a suggestion, trying to convince Tay.

Tay took his time to respond, having to process all this new info thoroughly.

"That shit sound too good to be true bro... We can go check it out, but we ain't just gon' expose our hand like that. Let's just go make ourselves known to the dude and see what he about first," he replied in a cool, condescending tone.

Then, just like that, his demeanor shifted from business to player mode after telling Miteous he'd catch up with him later. Tay was eager to get back to the new female that had just sparked his interest.

Miteous just shook his head and told him,

"Good luck with it. And don't forget about them jimmy hats that gramma gave you," suggesting Tay wear a condom.

They did their little handshake before parting ways.

When the school day ended, all Miteous wanted to do was find Tay and head downtown. But he couldn't, he had football practice.

Except when he got to the locker room to change, a sign was posted:

NO PRACTICE TODAY – PARENT-TEACHER CONFERENCES.

Most of the coaches were teachers, so practice was canceled.

Felt like it was meant to be.

Like the universe was clearing the way for them to explore this new business venture.

Miteous wondered if he could still catch up with Tay, knew he had to be somewhere close, and he knew just where to look.

After checking a couple of his honeycomb hideouts and still coming up empty, Miteous finally decided to head to Grannie's house before giving up on the search completely.

Grannie's, just around the corner from their school anyway.

Once Miteous got into Grannie's house through the back way Tay had shown him, he could hear noises coming from upstairs. He started wondering who else Tay might've shared the spot with, thinking maybe it was an uninvited guest.

Taking the stairs one at a time, leading up to the main room in the attic, the noises got louder and clearer. Miteous could tell there were at least two people up there now.

When he got to the door, he turned the knob slowly, trying to open it without alerting anyone to his presence.

That's when he saw the last thing he expected to see.

TayVaughn had taken Patrese to Grannie's house, and they were mid-session, she was on top of an old dresser, getting exactly what she came for, doggystyle, while Tay stood on his tippy toes, putting in work.

Tay finally turned around and saw Miteous sneaking up on them. The pair got startled and started scrambling for their clothes, pulling themselves together.

"Damn man, don'tchu know how to knock first, foo?" Tay said, irritated, but mostly trying to cover for Patrese's embarrassment. Then he smiled and winked at Miteous behind her back when she wasn't looking.

"My bad, bro. I thought somebody was in here that wasn't supposed to be," Miteous replied, trying to sound serious but also playing along.

"Whatchu doin' here anyway, bro? I thought you had practice or somethin' today?" Tay said, wondering why Miteous had even come to check the spot.

"I thought I did too, 'til I went to the locker room, and they said it was canceled due to parent-teacher conferences. So, I came by lookin' for you, to see if you was still tryna go see what was up wit ol' boy," Miteous replied, trying not to be overheard by Tay's company, nor look too long at her half-naked body as she got dressed.

That's when he realized it was the same girl he'd seen Tay hugged up with earlier in the hallway. He thought to himself, *Damn, they didn't waste no time.*

And not wanting to waste any more time wondering *what if,* they made their way downtown, dropping Patrese off on the way. They arrived at the pawn shop a short time later.

Exiting Tay's temporary transportation, as he liked to call it, and approaching the establishment, Miteous could tell just from the outside that there was a lot more going on in there than met the eye.

The place didn't give off any kind of inviting vibe. No colorful sign, no open hours, nothing that even said what kind of business it was. But to a criminally bent mind, that kind of discretion was gold.

Miteous was all the more eager to go inside. *Time to get paid.*

TayVaughn, on the other hand, noticed how quickly Miteous started moving, overly excited about the whole situation. He fell back a few steps and started scanning his surroundings, a habit he'd developed from growing up how he did.

Pulling out of a parallel parking space about a hundred yards away was an all-black SUV with blacked-out GMC rims and black tinted windows. Looked more like a secret service vehicle. It left in a hurry, but Tay didn't really pay it much mind, just made a mental note. It felt off.

Picking up his pace to catch up with Miteous, he said, "Damn nigga, slow down, this ain't no triathlon. I betchu ain't even see that, did you?"

He said it like a big brother schooling his little brother.

Miteous just looked at him puzzled, thinking about it, but not for too long. Tay was always putting him up on game. Not that Miteous wasn't sharp, he just didn't have the street sense Tay had from growing up in survival mode all day, every day. Miteous had more support, so he was blind to a lot of what Tay stayed alert to.

"Nah bro, I had somethin' in my eye. But watchu talkin' 'bout?" Miteous responded, brushing it off with an excuse.

Tay just shook his head and said, "That police-ass truck that just pulled off, that's what. But when we get in here, just back me up, bro, and let me do all the talkin'. I know these type of dudes. They always tryna feel you out to take you quick."

He looked Miteous dead in the eye to show he was serious. Miteous nodded in agreement as they approached the front door of the pawn shop. They opened it and stepped inside, hearing the bell jingle as the door closed behind them...

When Patrese got home, she couldn't wait to call up her best friend to tell her all about her latest escapade, getting bent over an old dresser in an abandoned house by TayVaughn, who gave her exactly what she'd been craving.

She had been feenin' for a young thug to seduce, and Tay delivered.

Her phone only rang a few times before her best friend picked up, but not in as good a mood.

"Hello," Chealsey said, sounding all pissed off.

"Damn girl, what's wrong witchu?" Patrese asked, immediately picking up on the vibe.

"Nothin' girl. Irritated. Tired of dealin' with deez no-good-ass niggas out here thinkin' a bitch was born yesterday and shit," Chealsey snapped, with more bite now that she had someone to vent to.

"What that nigga done did now, girl? Do we gotta go slash some tires and bust some windows? Cause you know a bitch gotcho back, right?" Patrese said, reassuring her.

"Nah, not yet. I jus' caught the nigga in other bitches' DMs. But this him callin' me back now, lemme call you right back. I gotta set this nigga straight real quick," she said, then hung up.

CHAPTER 7

The next morning when Tony and Mike linked up again, Tony was heated. He'd lost another expensive bracelet at the strip club last night, and since it was the third one this year, it was starting to cut into his profit margins. Even though he was completely hammered, he still couldn't figure out how this kept happening.

Trying not to let this little problem distract him from his much bigger ones, he made up his mind right then to cut his losses and start paying more attention, before he let this dumb shit throw his whole day off.

Snapping out of it, he remembered what was really at stake. The move had gone the complete opposite of what they planned, and now they were in a bit of a conundrum.

That's when Tony got a bright idea while he was driving and ran it past Mike, just to hear how it sounded out loud.

"Ey, what about yo cousin that be sellin' all dem guns to people? I know he come across somethin' new every day. U wanna go check out his inventory?" Tony asked after some deep contemplation.

"Yea, fuck it. Let's just roll up on him. Cuz most guns, u can't tell apart if it's the same make and model. We gotta go see for ourselves, it's been a min since I stopped by there anyway," Mike replied, actually liking the idea as soon as he heard it. He was just happy Tony finally came up with *something*, 'cause riding around in awkward silence while trying to think of one himself was gettin' old fast.

They pulled up to Mike's cousin Randy's spot, a one-bedroom apartment in a complex the locals called *The Towers* because of its tall, compact brick structure, stacking one resident's unit right on top of the next.

After entering through the lobby and riding the stale-smelling elevator, they got off and walked down the hallway toward Randy's apartment. But once they got to the door, a whole new stench hit them.

Mike knocked loud enough to be heard by the neighbors while Tony stood behind him, looking up and down the hallway for signs of life. But there was no movement. Nobody came to the door.

Growing concerned, Mike reached for the doorknob and twisted it, realizing it had been unlocked the whole time. He felt kind of slow for not checking first but still didn't wanna be rude or intrusive. He stepped inside slowly, calling out Randy's name with every step, trying to make his presence known so Randy wouldn't accidentally shoot him, knowing he always kept a gun close by.

But the smell got worse the deeper they moved inside.

Mike's instincts kicked in. Something was off.

Out of paranoia, he pulled his gun. Tony did the same, following close behind him, both of them moving like experienced cops canvassing an area for a suspect. They crept through the apartment with stealth, still not hearing a peep from Randy, or even a TV on too loud for that matter.

Once they reached the narrow hallway past the living room, they decided to split up. One door led to the bedroom, the other to the bathroom. Mike, growing more tense by the second, went toward the bedroom. Tony took the bathroom.

Both doors were closed, but the smell was definitely coming from nearby.

Mike opened the bedroom door first since it was closest. Randy wasn't in there.

That's when he turned around and heard Tony call for help from the bathroom.

Holstering his weapon at the small of his back, Mike rushed in.

He found his cousin unconscious, a needle sticking out of his arm. Blue-faced. No signs of life left in him.

Cold.

Mike had known Randy used heroin from time to time, but always thought of him as a functioning addict, somebody who still handled business while getting high. But in reality, Randy had lost control as soon as the drugs let go. And this time, the hit he took was a blast there was no coming back from.

Looking around and finding no signs of a struggle, or any evidence of someone else having been there, they decided to search the apartment for anything illegal before calling it in. Mike wanted to spare the rest of the family the sleepless nights of wondering what else Randy might've been into that could've led to his death.

Especially since Randy still had a good image in the family's eyes after serving in the military when he was younger.

Randy was a few years younger than Mike, which made him around 33. He never had kids or a serious relationship after being drafted at 18. He stayed alone, and he was never quite the same after returning from overseas. That's probably where the drug abuse started.

Socially awkward, no one really bothered with him, except Mike.

And now Mike was overwhelmed with a flood of emotions. Exiting the bathroom, he wiped his face and took a deep breath before he commenced the final shakedown of his cousin's residence.

He was really gonna miss him.

Mike thought about their last interaction, Randy going on and on about how he was gonna travel the world once he saved up enough money. Never thought his days would end this soon.

But that's how the cookie crumbled sometimes. Here today, gone the next. No warnings. No happy endings. No goodbyes.

While rummaging through the apartment, Tony and Mike came across several firearms, as expected. They also found some old army photos of Randy with his platoon and team leaders.

Then inside Randy's closet, stashed inside three different pairs of sneakers, they found crisp stacks of hundreds, totaling $53,000. Tony made Mike aware of it. They assumed it was money Randy had been saving for his trip.

They split it up between them.

After loading everything into a duffel bag, Mike headed to the door to call in the overdose. But then he remembered Randy always being secretive about an attic space above his linen closet.

He just had to check it before leaving the place for the last time.

Mike sent Tony ahead to load everything into the car and said he'd catch up. Grabbing a kitchen chair, he dragged it over to the closet, stood on top of it, and opened the attic door.

Holding the lid ajar with one hand, he reached around with the other, it was too dark to see anything up there. He pushed his whole arm in, feeling around for anything out of place. After about five minutes of searching, he was about to give up when he touched some insulation that felt lumpier than the rest.

He grabbed a handful and pulled it up.

Sitting in a perfectly molded groove was a little black duffel bag, looked like it could've held one of those handheld camcorders or something.

He pulled it down and started digging through it.

Unzipping the bag, he saw a bunch of papers.

Not having time to sit there and read through them, he decided to take them with him. He exited the apartment and went to catch up with Tony, who had to be getting impatient by now.

Pulling out his phone on the way out, Mike called in an accidental overdose…

The next day, Booker woke up bright and early to head to the pawn shop and meet up with his hired help, Oliver Maxwell. Standing at six-foot-five and weighing well over three hundred pounds, Oliver had once gotten stuck behind a desk at Langley, not that it surprised him. As big of a force as he was physically, he couldn't see worth a damn. The man wore bifocal spectacles he kept readjusting on his face 'cause they never fit right, which ultimately led to his military discharge once his eyesight started failing in his later years.

But what he lacked in vision, he made up for in IQ.

Oliver graduated top of his class at every level, since his first graduation, and even by the highest standards, was considered a brilliant analyst. Having served over 30 years in military and government vocations, he was one of the best they'd ever had. The man could access nearly any piece of information on anyone, from any time, if it had ever been officially uploaded or physically documented in any national database.

He was as dangerous as they came when it came to what he could do with the right information in his hands, and everything he already knew. That's why he never made superiors, clients, or competitors uncomfortable. He guaranteed complete confidentiality in contracts… signed in actual blood. Then he'd burn them after snapping a Polaroid for his own private collection.

He was one lonely, vicious, mean grunt, especially after losing the one good thing he had left in life: his wife, who died of cancer three years ago.

Still, he was a great asset to keep on call.

Booker had only hired him once before in the past but was satisfied with his work. So, despite their long personal history, going all the way back to high school before life took them down separate paths, Booker decided to use him again.

After navigating through morning traffic, Booker finally pulled up to the shop early, where Oliver was already waiting out front in his latest model Tahoe. All blacked out, rims, tint, everything. Looked like one of Will Smith's cars from *Men in Black*, way too police-looking for this side of town.

Booker pulled up beside him and signaled for him to roll his window down.

"Man, u lookin' like the police and shit out here. Start parking down the street a lil' ways, you blowin' up my spot, I still got a business to run," he said.

Oliver just smiled and gave a thumbs up before starting the engine and doing exactly what he was told.

They got out of their vehicles and walked up to the front of the establishment. Booker pulled out his keys and opened up the shop. As they moved through the small corridors into the back office, which was nearly the same size as the front area, it was clear who had the ego. The man took up just as much space as he didn't need.

"Breath out my body, only time I can't get a meal, Jack. You feel me?" Booker said arrogantly, sparking up a Cuban and offering one to his guest.

"I can understand that my friend," Oliver replied, accepting the gesture, clipping the tip and lighting his cigar. "But I'm curious to know what task demands my services this time."

Booker exhaled a thick cloud of smoke, adding to the drama before speaking in his most sophisticated voice.

"Well, I got these two guys that been workin' for me, right? And it appears they've been disloyal. Now, I can't prove nothin' right now, which is why they still breathin' and employed. It's all speculation. I can't always be at two places at once and keep an eye on everything. So, I need you to monitor them for me for a few weeks. Let me know what you come up with, see if you catch any suspicious activity. I'll pay you five grand. How's that sound?"

"That don't sound like a problem at all, my friend," Oliver replied smoothly. "But make it even, and I'll even help you come up with a real simple solution, *if* I happen to confirm your suspicions. You know my work."

Then came that deep-chested smoker's cough.

Booker nodded, glad Oliver didn't charge him the same ten up front as last time. They shook on it.

Oliver brought out his pen and pad and started jotting down the specific information he needed to get started, looking like a waiter at a five-star restaurant making sure he got the order just right. He pulled out a contract, had Booker sign it, took a Polaroid, and burned it.

Business concluded, for now.

Changing the subject to something more personal, Oliver started reminiscing.

"Remember back in the day when I was first gettin' started and you had that problem with them one dudes, uh huh…"

But before he could finish, Booker's phone started ringing from the table between them.

The more he tried to ignore it, the louder it seemed to get. Ringing. And ringing.

Booker finally picked up.

"Hello, Booker's Pawn, Loans, and Sells. How may I help you?" he answered, switching into his professional tone.

Smacking into the receiver with attitude, a familiar voice snapped back.

"Uh-huh, I *knew* yo ass was there. Wait, you can't answer yo phone now? Nigga, wat lil' bitch u over there entertainin' today that gotchu ignorin' me?" Patrese barked.

She was pissed he hadn't answered his cell or responded to any of the nasty pics she sent him, ones that usually got his full and undivided attention. She'd sent them confidently, knowing he'd be ready to do whatever she needed.

"Naw babe, I ain't even been able to check my phone yet," Booker said, soft-spoken now, trying to keep the conversation discreet. "I was just finishin' up a business meeting with an old friend, so just' calm down. I was just makin' plans to come see you today after I wrap this up. How's that sound?"

"Yea, okay," she said, her tone flipping from hostile to flirty in a heartbeat. "I'll be ready in a few hours. And u gon' like what I just' sent too. Just' wait and see..."

Booker smirked, then changed his tone back to all business before ending the call, pretending like it was just another work-related thing in front of Oliver, who wasn't dumb or intrusive, just observant.

They made a little more small talk. Then Oliver stubbed out his cigar and exited Booker's office, promising to stop by once or twice a week with updates.

Booker, now alone, hurried to pull out his cell to check the messages and missed calls from Patrese. He figured it was a good time to get to the next order of business for the day: satisfying his own sick and lustful desires.

Taking advantage of a young sex addict who made him feel young again... while he provided her with everything older women took for granted...

CHAPTER 8

"Come on in the back, fellas," Miteous and Tay heard a baritone voice call out from the office area in the far east corner of the pawn shop right as they stepped through the front entrance.

Figuring they were on camera was the only way the man could've seen them before they saw him. They kept walking straight past the store area, heading toward the voice, eyes scanning the shelves full of all kinds of wild merch the owner had collected over the years.

Out of the corners of their eyes, they peeped all sorts of antique shit, old guns, dusty jewelry, rusted worker tools, and tried not to judge the book by its cover. But truthfully, the place could've used a real upgrade. Even though it smelled like freshly dried paint, it looked like it hadn't been swept or mopped in months.

If Miteous had to describe the pawn shop in one word, it would've been "front." 'Cause whatever money the owner was makin' to keep the lights on, it damn sure wasn't coming from any legit nine-to-five, Monday-through-Friday hustle. Not in *those* conditions. No way.

They made their own judgments walking in and finally reached the back, where it was time to meet the man in charge and find out what was really going on.

Seated behind a big mahogany desk was the man they'd come to see. They took a seat across from him, now face-to-face with the man of the hour.

"Name's Booker. I own the place. Now, what can I help you two gentlemen out with today?" Booker said in a serious but chill tone, lighting up a cigar and blowing smoke in their direction.

Tay was the first to speak, just like they planned. He looked at Miteous, cool and confident like he had it under control.

"Nice to meetchu, man. My name Tay Vaughn, and this my brother-from-another-mother, Miteous. We go to school with Sammy, who tells us that chu may be into fencin'… if it's worthy, o' course," Tay said, laying down the reason for their visit as sincerely as he could.

"Yeah, go ahead," Booker replied, like he wasn't denying it, but also letting it be known it wasn't really their business.

Sensing that, Tay kept going.

"And like I was sayin', me and my bro be performin' odd jobs, meanin' thefts and burglaries, and we always comin' across some high-quality shit we could really flip if we had somebody like you as our sponsor. So, I was wonderin' if we could propose a deal… go into business together."

He said it with the kind of confidence that made it sound like the cards were stacked in *his* favor.

Booker leaned in after that last part, intrigued by these two young, hungry hustlers. They were on a different maturity level than most kids their age. He could sense their street knowledge and grind. It reminded him of when Tony and Mike were first gettin' started, back when he'd taken them in, raised them up like sons. It pained him to be where things were with them now.

But looking at these two, he started seriously considering them as replacements… if things worked out.

"And what do you propose the terms of our little arrangement should be?" Booker asked, leaning forward. "But before you answer, I'm only gonna give you one shot at this, so choose your terms wisely… or you could miss out on an opportunity of a lifetime."

He added that last part to apply pressure, just to see how they'd handle it. He was already testing Tay.

Tay glanced at Miteous for a quick confidence boost and got it with a simple head nod, *you got this*.

"Well, I was thinkin' about a seventy-thirty split. Considerin' the fact that we gon' split the seventy at thirty-five apiece… basically, we *all* get the same slice of the pie, with a lil' extra off the top for bringin' you good, consistent business on high-quality items only. Sixty-forty when *you* pick the spot or put us on a lick. How's that sound?"

He laid it down with full confidence. Not a single hesitation in tone or pitch.

If Booker had to admit it, he was impressed. The duo was solid, and he could use a few more hungry soldiers on the night shift. Agreeably, he stuck out his hand.

"Sounds like you've got yourselves a fence, young man. I'm lookin' forward to a profitable future witchu. And if I come across some extra errands I need done on the side, I'll be in touch. So just leave behind some contact info, and I'll get ahold of yaw. And if yaw happen to have somethin' for me and I'm not here, contact this number, I'll be sure to get back witchu," Booker said, handing them a card with his personal number on it.

Tay Vaughn took it. They shook hands, sealing the business arrangement.

Then Booker turned to Miteous.

"Man of a few words, huh?" he asked, trying to get a feel for him too.

"All about that action. But I'm sure we will speak again," Miteous replied, making sure not to undermine his best friend's authority by showin' off his own just yet.

Booker noticed it and was overly impressed by the loyalty and respect the two shared. That kind of bond was rare in this game, especially at their age. He could tell they'd known each other a long time. It takes a long time to get that kind of rhythm with someone. He knew then he'd made the right call bringin' them into his operation, even if they were lower level than his usual players.

Everybody gotta start somewhere. And if these two stayed down with him, they'd rise through the ranks real quick.

Concluding their business and leaving the shop, Miteous and Tay exchanged a handshake of congratulations once they got back to the car. Everything had gone just like they planned. They could already feel their pockets gettin' heavier and their financial stress gettin' lighter.

They were proving to themselves they *could* do this, as long as they stuck together and stayed focused on the mission. And now that they had a sponsor in a solid position, it was time to prove their worth the only way that mattered, by puttin' in work.

Tay put the car in drive and headed to a remote location where he already had a lick lined up. He'd done his homework.

With everything running smoothly at Booker's, and football season coming to a close, Miteous started thinking about jumping into his side career full-time. Money was becoming the most important thing in his life, it made the world go 'round, and it motivated everybody to move, work, plot, and grind to get it.

It could literally *buy* the happiness you were searching for... by giving you time to do what you wanted, as long as you wanted, with whoever you wanted.

And Miteous had things he wanted to do with his time.

Still dating Veronica, still tryin' to keep up with the latest trends, it all cost. And he felt he needed *more* of it to keep feelin' that bliss. That self-fulfillment.

But being fearlessly ambitious comes with a price... especially when you don't see the caution signs on the road ahead.

And Miteous would end up learning that lesson the hard way, when he turned down an outlet one day... that could've been his last.

It was a Friday night, just as routine as any other, but all throughout the day, Miteous had been extra eager to get through it. Usually, gametime was the highlight of his Fridays, but not this one. This night was different.

And it doesn't really matter what the experience is, people never forget the first time they experience something *for the first time*. Neither could Miteous. Because this Friday night, he experienced *several* firsts.

His first came *during* the game. Miteous hit a state of choiceless awareness for the first time.

They were going up against their school rivals, and the pressure was on heavy. Down by three points, third down, six yards to go. His coach sent him in with a play, and Miteous already knew, he was getting the ball. This one was his.

He took a deep breath to calm the anxiety, thinking about all the drills, training, and reps that brought him to this moment. He knew he was ready. Knew he could flip the game around. And right then, a calm confidence washed over him, something he'd never felt before.

He relayed the play to the quarterback, who broke the huddle and signaled everyone to get in position. The QB lined up under center, the fullback behind him, and Miteous in the back, forming that classic I-formation.

All Miteous could feel was adrenaline rushing through his veins.

Then, it happened.

Everything disappeared. The noise. The pressure. The crowd. It was like seeing with new eyes, *pure clarity*. Total awareness. He saw *everything*.

"Hike!" the QB shouted.

Faking a handoff to the fullback, the quarterback then slipped the ball into Miteous' arms cleanly. One hand over, one under, the proper running back form. Ball tucked tight, he scanned the field like a hawk.

Right in front of him, a gap opened up between the guard and tackle. He made his first move, planted his foot hard and cut sharp toward the sideline.

A linebacker lunged. Missed.

Miteous hit the sideline in full stride. The crowd was on their feet.

Zoning in was a free safety, the last line of defense.

Miteous kept a steady pace, patient, eyes locked. Then, just before the safety could explode into a diving tackle, Miteous *stopped*. The safety flew right past, crashed into the sideline.

Miteous cut back, untouched, and crossed into the end zone.

Touchdown. Game over.

The crowd exploded. His team went wild.

Miteous had just sealed the win with the best play of his season, *maybe* of his entire high school career. It was one for the books. None of his teammates, or anyone who saw it, would ever forget.

And the night… was still young.

After the big win came the real celebration. Miteous and his team liked to party just as hard as they practiced. And word was already spreading fast about a senior's party. Everyone on the team was invited.

Miteous figured it'd be the perfect opportunity to bring Tay along, and maybe case a few houses afterward. He knew the area: nice neighborhood, rich folks, false sense of security. Prime setup. Somebody *was* gonna get caught slippin'.

He hit the locker room, showered fast, and called Tay to set the play in motion.

Then he headed to the school parking lot, which was already packed out like a tailgate party. Cars coming and going, people rallying up. That's when he spotted Tay, parked in the corner, laid low in some old-school Acura that looked like a work car somebody was *definitely* gonna be pissed about losing in the morning.

Miteous slid into the passenger seat and peeped Tay already in stealth mode. All black everything. Black gloves. Tactical as hell.

"Damn, man," Miteous said, half-laughing. "I said case a couple houses *after* the party. You lookin' like Martin Lawrence off *Blue Streak* when he robbed that jewelry store, bro. The whole point of hittin' the party first is so our alibi's solid. If anything, go wrong out there, we got a bunch of folks sayin' exactly what we need 'em to."

It was Miteous' turn to school him, like old times. That's what made them so dangerous together.

"That's why I got so much love for you, my nigga," Tay said, laughing. "Cuz you square, and you ain't got one care."

He leaned back in his seat, smiling real easy now. No fear. Just comfort. He knew he had someone in his corner for real. And in his lifestyle, that was everything.

Miteous wasn't just smart, he had vision. He could see *outside* the box, and that gave him a different kind of perspective in high-pressure situations.

But even a fool knows everything... except his *own* ignorance.

Tay, switching the subject from his tactical gear, started teasing.

"Man, I still can't believe you ran into Veronica again *before* me. That's crazy," he said, half-joking. But lowkey, he was jealous. Veronica was fine.

"Yeah, whatever, nigga. Can't fight fate. Cards fall how they may," Miteous shot back. "You just worry 'bout keepin' Ms. *Ebony* right down there in the *Projects*."

He said it with extra emphasis on *Projects*, poking fun in return.

A short drive later, they pulled up to the party. Cars lined both sides of the street, jammed up. Looked like a full house.

They circled a couple times before finally finding a parking spot safe enough, but still close enough to walk, which was like finding a needle in a haystack.

Tay changed his clothes right there in the car, to look more like a partygoer.

As soon as they got a little way from the car, Tay's phone started ringing. He fell back a few steps and told Miteous, "Go head and check the party out without me, bro. I'ma catch up."

Miteous nodded and kept walking while Tay returned to the whip to take the call.

"Hello," he said smooth and slow into the receiver, trying to sound like a straight-up player.

It was Ebony on the line.

"Hey daddy. I just called to tell you I ran into Alibimac today, and he said since things been running so smoothly with you holdin' down his trap, he got somethin' for you. Told me to tell you to get at him tomorrow," she said, trying to sound like a sexy secretary.

"Aight then, that's what's up. We makin' strides. I been waitin' to level up on that side anyway. Good lookin' out, babe," Tay said, his voice dipping into seduction. "Now what you got on right now?"

She flipped the script and seduced him instead. "Uh, right now? I got your favorite outfit on… and you gon' see it when you get here, *if* you comin' over tonight, that is."

"Hell yeah, if that's yo invitation, I ain't gon' be long. Just gotta hit a couple spots with my guy real quick," he said, actin' like he had to explain himself.

He hung up not long after, and by the time he got to the front entrance of the party, Miteous was already headed back out, sweaty and outta breath like he'd just run a damn marathon.

"Girls can't get enough of me, bro! Go in there, it's straight poppin'!" Miteous said, having just finished grindin' on every chick who wanted to dance in the last twenty minutes.

Tay got curious, nodded, and went in too.

About an hour later, both of them came stumbling out of the party, tired, sweaty, and out of breath, but satisfied they'd made their presence felt.

Time for the next move: scouting houses.

They cruised through the luxurious neighborhood, looking for any security flaws. But it seemed like they waited too late, all the houses were blacked out, lights off inside and out, garages shut.

So, they dipped to the neighborhood next to it, just across the roundabout and through the turnpike, to see what was crackin' over there.

That's when Tay slammed on the brakes.

"Damn!" he said, eyes locked on something. He threw the car in reverse, backing up a few blocks like he just snapped outta a daydream.

He whipped the car down a side street and stopped in front of a house with a familiar vehicle parked in the driveway.

"That's the truck I was talkin' about from the other day, bro," Tay said, tapping Miteous on the shoulder and pointing.

Miteous stared at the vehicle, even though he didn't recognize it. But he wanted to help Tay, so he played along.

"Whatchu want me to do, bro? Go knock on the door and ask for somebody we know damn well don't live there?"

Tay couldn't shake the feeling. He had to know who was in that house.

He gave Miteous the go-ahead, to see if anybody was home, to try and feel 'em out.

Seemed like a good idea at the time.

Miteous got out the car, walked past the two-car garage, and peeped that there weren't any cameras. That was always a green light in his line of work.

He walked up to the front door, knocked, and stood there waiting.

Standing in the heat of the night, a chill ran down his spine. The hairs on the back of his neck stood up.

But he brushed it off…

Just after midnight, Oliver Maxwell was back at his place.

After getting his assignment from Booker, he went home to do his preliminary assessment on the two young men he'd been hired to watch.

Oliver prided himself on preparation. Always did. It's what made him dangerous and always delivered the best possible results.

And now that he lived alone, still mourning the death of his wife, his only companion of 22 years, he had *nothing but time*. Time to think. Time to work. Which meant *trouble* for whoever he was watching.

This man was *ruthlessly relentless* when it came to gathering intelligence. He'd figure out your schedule, your habits, your paper trail. He didn't miss *anything.*

Sitting at his high-tech computer station, he had access to encrypted files, government databases, and his old FBI clearance. He ran his private investigation firm as a front, but it gave him reach like you wouldn't believe.

Typing away, he pulled up medical records, criminal histories, financial reports, and IP addresses. He could track your devices down to the exact place they got online.

Like Nev off *Catfish*. But faster. And ten times more dangerous.

He scribbled in his notepad, flagging anomalies worth digging into. Some of it might lead him straight to answers. Other things? Maybe a whole lot more.

After several hours of deep work, he finally called it quits. Leaned back, stretched, and that's when he saw it.

Lights flashed across his window. A car pulling into his driveway.

He hadn't lived at that house long, just moved in before his wife passed. Bought it as a retirement gift for them both. It was common for people to get lost in that neighborhood. The layout was a maze.

He figured it was someone who took a wrong turn.

But then…

A *door shut*.

Then… *a knock*.

Oliver froze.

He hadn't invited *anybody*. He hadn't even given out his new address.

Paranoia kicked in hard. Years of black ops and shadow dealings made his mind snap into survival mode.

He grabbed his Glock .40 from a hidden compartment in his nightstand, crept downstairs, and approached the front door.

Through the living room window, he saw a figure standing there.

Dark clothes. Still. Quiet. Didn't look familiar at all.

Oliver raised his voice.

"You're trespassing on private property! Leave now!"

The figure didn't move. Didn't say a word. Just stood there… like they were waiting.

Waiting for something.

Oliver felt the danger rise.

Paranoia gripped him tight, and he *snapped.*

He raised his gun and started *firing through the door.*

Bullets ripped through the wood, shattered glass, and blasted through walls. Hollow points tore the space to pieces, debris flew everywhere.

By the time he reached the door, expecting to call in a homicide…

Nobody was there.

Nobody.

He couldn't believe it. He couldn't see worth a damn, but he'd been *too close* to have missed.

Whoever that kid was… wasn't just blessed.

He was amazingly *fast.*

Oliver had never seen someone outrun a bullet, no matter how big of a head start they had.

CHAPTER 9

The next day, Tony and Mike linked up again, right after hearing about Randy's death and seeing all the stuff at his place that might explain how he ended up that way. They decided to head to one of their trap houses and go over everything with a fine-tooth comb.

Mike had found a bunch of papers they needed to sift through, try to piece together what actually happened. The scene had been *way* too staged for Mike to feel settled about his cousin supposedly OD'ing like that. It just didn't add up.

Pulling into the garage, Tony went through his usual routine. He never left his car outside in drug-infested neighborhoods, not for long, not even by accident. He'd been carjacked once before and wasn't tryin' to let that happen again.

All the whips he got through the dealership came with trackers and top-tier alarm systems. He even got tight when somebody touched his car, left fingerprints, or just *looked* at it too long. Saying he was a car junkie was putting it lightly, especially when it came to his Benz. Dude treated it like Bo's GTO off *Dukes of Hazzard*. Just too attached.

Meanwhile, Mike went upstairs to grab everything and came back down with two big duffle bags like they'd just come back from a recovery mission or military op.

He set the bags down between them and pulled up two plastic chairs. There was a table nearby in case they needed to lay stuff out for closer inspection. But before they could even get started...

Tony's phone rang.

He looked at Mike, puzzled, not expecting nobody to hit him at that time.

Mike just shot him a look like, *"Nigga, don't look at me. That's your phone, I don't know what you got goin' on."*

Tony checked the caller ID, saw the familiar digits, and instantly knew it was the Bossman. He answered like any man in his position would.

"Wassup, Boss? What's goin' on?" Tony asked, way less enthusiastic than usual, sounded almost hesitant, like he already knew this wasn't just a check-in call.

"I need y'all to come by the shop today," Booker said straight up. "I got a job for y'all. Somethin' came up and I need it handled *immediately.* That gon' be a problem?"

"Nah, not a problem at all, Bossman. We on our way," Tony answered quickly, stumbling over his words a little, sensing this was serious. He didn't want to push back or say the wrong thing.

As soon as he hung up, Mike went off.

"Man, what Booker old ass want with us now?" Mike said. "And why was you soundin' all *soft* on the phone when you was talkin' to that nigga?"

Tony looked at him, face tightening.

"Nigga, ain't nobody soundin' soft. This chess, not checkers. It's called playin' possum," he snapped. "His old ass said he got a job for us, and he need it done *today.* Told us to stop by as soon as possible. So, we gon' have to wrap this shit up and come back to it later. He *expectin'* us."

That was the G talking now. Unapologetically.

They made a few stops on the way to Booker's, grabbed some food, ran a few errands, then finally parked out front of the pawn shop.

As soon as they walked in, they could smell that expensive-ass cigar smoke and knew Booker was in his office.

"Have a seat, gentlemen. Let me talk to y'all about a few things real quick before I tell you what the job is," Booker said, puffing away on his cigar, studying every movement and facial expression they made like a lie detector test.

Tony and Mike sat down, feeling the pressure.

"I didn't tell y'all I received another shipment this afternoon. We'll address that other little situation later... but right now, I need proof of y'all's locations from about six to eight hours ago," Booker said coldly.

"And if y'all *can't* account for y'all's whereabouts... I'ma take that as a sign of war. And we won't have *any* more business to discuss, *ever.*"

Tony and Mike looked at each other like, *What the fuck?*

They couldn't afford to lose their spot in Booker's operation. So, without hesitation, they pulled out their phones and showed him everything, timestamps, locations, proof. No questions asked.

Booker looked it over, then leaned back. Seemed satisfied. His tone cooled a little.

Mike was the first to speak up.

"No disrespect, Bossman… but what is all this *really* about anyway? What's goin' on?" he asked, sincerely. The look in his eyes told Booker they were just as lost as he was mad.

Booker nodded slowly.

"Like I was sayin', since our last… misunderstanding, I ain't told y'all yet that we had a load come in. Y'all was gonna have to increase y'all runner's amount this month. *Double it.* So, while y'all was out handlin' that business I gave y'all… I called in y'all Capo to handle the rest. And one of 'em got robbed. Killed this afternoon."

He paused. Blew out a thick cloud of smoke.

"And it just so happens to be someone that reports directly to y'all."

He looked up and said it:

"Alibimac."

Booker leaned in, eyes on them both.

But what he saw surprised him.

It wasn't guilt.

It was *shock*. Deep concern. Anger. Genuine disbelief.

They hadn't known.

Booker knew then, he was wrong about Tony and Mike. Whatever conspiracy he'd started to build in his head got debunked that moment.

But now?

A new question formed.

If not *them*... then *who*?

After barely escaping with his life, Miteous had a *lot* on his mind. This life he was living... it was catching up to him fast. Everything he'd been building, his girl, his money, his moves, was on the line.

He hardly got any sleep that night. His subconscious kept dragging him back to the moment it almost all went south.

He thought about his mom. What would've happened if she got a call saying her son had been killed?

He didn't want to go there. Wouldn't let his mind stay on it, it was just too painful.

But getting shot at for the first time changed something in him. Whether it was for better or worse, he wasn't sure. But it made him *aware*, he was expendable.

He couldn't just keep diving headfirst into deep water without knowing what was underneath.

It wasn't until he got back to the car and Tay drove off that it really hit him.

He was *close, real close* to death.

And it wasn't until Tay apologized for the thirtieth time that he realized just how much love he had for that boy. He had *never* seen Tay that vulnerable before. Never had to consider the possibility that his best friend in the whole world almost got killed over a stupid hunch.

It hit him in the chest. Hard.

But it also solidified something between them.

A bond.

For life.

The next day, Miteous woke up earlier than usual, partly because he heard his sister sneaking into his room to play her computer games, partly to escape his idle thoughts, and mostly to get started on his chores so he could go do what he wanted afterward.

That usually meant yard work: making sure the grass was cut and every leaf that fell was cleared before his dad came home to inspect it. One less reason for him to say no whenever Miteous asked for something he really needed, or somewhere he really wanted to go. That's just how his parents' system worked, and he knew how to navigate it all too well.

By the time he finished his duties and took a shower, Tay was pulling up on him, asking if he could come along to take care of some business real quick. Promised him he'd pick their girls up afterward, take them to the mall, and catch a movie, *on him*, especially when he sensed Miteous wasn't feelin' it.

Not wanting to let Tay down, but not really trying to entertain anything *felonious* either, Miteous reluctantly agreed… mostly because he really wanted to see his girl. But he *definitely* regretted getting in the car.

No matter how much he was looking forward to spending some quality time with his girl, especially after coming out of that last debacle untouched, he really needed some intimate companionship right now to ease his mind and frustrations. So, he hopped in, and they drove off.

"Where we goin', anyway, bro?" Miteous asked as soon as his door closed. "Cause after last night, my nigga… that shit got me on edge."

Leaning back in his seat, relaxed and levelheaded, Tay replied, "Aw man, you still thinkin' 'bout that shit? That day done came and went. We just 'bout to go grab some shit from my guy, then we gon' go get on these females. Straight up. It ain't gon' take that long, bro. Just sit back and relax, we chillin' today."

Satisfied with Tay's answer, reading his body language and tone, Miteous let his guard down. Tay sounded casual, like this was just another regular errand. He'd taken Miteous along for thousands of those. So Miteous adjusted his seat and leaned it all the way back, tryin' to relax.

About 45 minutes later, they pulled up to what looked like an abandoned tire shop, something off an old highway. The sign on top was so worn down that it had letters missing, looked like it used to read "Auto Body Tires and Repairs."

Tay was first to get out, parking a little ways away like he always did. He told Miteous he could come if he wanted.

That's when Miteous looked over and noticed the butt of a gun sticking out the small of Tay's back. His shirt had lifted a little as he moved. Tay quickly pulled it down to cover it, trying to be discreet.

Miteous didn't say anything, figured maybe it was just a precaution from the other night, but he *definitely* noted that Tay was strapped.

They entered the building, Miteous not far behind.

Inside, it was full of crates and boxes everywhere, it looked like somebody bought the old shop and turned it into some kind of storage unit. There were still a few car lifts in place, used for raising up vehicles so mechanics could work underneath. The place still smelled like oil, rubber, and metal.

Walking toward the back of the tire shop, Tay finally spotted his guy, the one they came to see. They greeted each other like old homies.

"Wassup, big money," Alibimac said to his prodigy. He'd been training Tay to run things for him one day. He really liked Tay and saw potential in him.

He was moving boxes from one spot to another as Miteous and Tay walked into the enclosed area he'd been turning into his little office space. Alibimac was short, dark-skinned, maybe 5'8" but well over 200 pounds, most of its lean muscle. Looked like he used to be athletic back in the day. Kept his haircut low and rocked color-coordinated designer fits like it was second nature.

"Tryna get like *you*, big time," Tay joked back. "It's yo' world, and I'm just a squirrel tryna get a nut."

They laughed and dapped up.

That's when Alibimac looked over at Miteous.

"Who ya boy?" he asked, not concerned, just curious.

"Oh, my bad. This my main man Miteous, trust him with my life," Tay said, making it clear he was vouching heavily.

Then he turned to Miteous. "Miteous, this one of the hardest hustlers in the game and my business partner, Alibimac."

"Nice to meet you, man," Miteous said, nodding and shaking his hand before falling back to let them talk business.

That's when the vibe *changed*.

Suddenly, you could cut the tension in the room with a butter knife.

Miteous didn't know the specifics of their previous dealings, but whatever it was, Tay wasn't feelin' it. He kept referring back to their last agreement, and Alibimac kept pushing different terms, trying to get more money out of Tay for his re-up.

Tay said that with Alibimac's new terms, he wouldn't make any profit. Felt like he was being treated more like a servant than a business partner, especially after running his trap for weeks.

Before Miteous could even piece it all together to try and mediate, the tension exploded. Tay and Alibimac got up in each other's faces, voices raised, the argument growing more aggressive by the second.

Then, outta nowhere, Alibimac lost his cool.

He cocked his hand back and *clocked* Tay in the jaw, sending him stumbling into a stack of boxes.

And *before* Miteous could even react...

BANG.

The room went *silent*.

You could've heard a pin drop.

Miteous looked down.

Blood poured from Alibimac's forehead like a busted pipe. Dead center between his eyes. Tay stood over him, blank expression, gun still smoking in his hand.

"Man, dude... what'd you just do?" Miteous said, snapping Tay outta his trance.

"I... I don't know, bro. Shit happened so quick... that nigga was tryna get over, tryna play me sweet. Then he socked me in my shit, and I was so mad I just... I just..." Tay said, trailing off again, staring at Alibimac's body lying there stiff in a growing pool of blood, wondering how it all went left so fast.

He couldn't even think straight.

Miteous, seeing this, switched into survival mode like he had many times before, for both of them.

"Aight then, this what we gon' do, bro," Miteous said firmly. "First, give me the gun."

Tay looked him in the eyes, then handed it over.

Miteous took the weapon, pulled the hammer back, and shot Alibimac *again*, in a different spot, one Tay couldn't see.

"Now we all the way locked in this shit *together*," Miteous said, eyes locked on Tay's.

That mutual understanding between them didn't need any explanation.

Then Miteous told Tay to check the box that fell over, he thought he'd seen something in it.

Tay looked.

Inside was several ounces of white powder and several more of weed.

They grabbed that too.

Then they checked Alibimac's pockets, took everything of value or that could tie them to the scene. Found a phone, a fat wad of cash, took all of it.

Before leaving, Tay suggested they wipe down everything they could've touched. They cleaned what they could, then bounced.

They headed straight to Tay's temporary ride.

New destination: Granny's house.

CHAPTER 10

Once Tony and Mike got the news about Alibimac's demise, they devised a plan to catch the culprit, whoever it may have been, by taking over his territory themselves and dealing directly with his day-to-day clientele.

They figured that hitting the streets he used to run might bring out some info from somebody who'd seen or heard something, especially if someone recently came up on a lot of high-quality drugs they didn't have before. And now that Tony and Mike had the product, they knew they had to sell it somewhere in order to make it worth the trouble. So, they laid out a little safety net, hoping to catch wind of something... anything... that could lead them in the right direction.

Avenging their longtime friend's murder, somebody who'd been loyal to them from the start, had to take a backseat for now. First, they needed to head back to their own trap and finish sorting through everything they'd found in Randy's apartment.

It seemed like every time they turned around, somebody they knew was getting killed. And for whatever reason, it felt like their responsibility to bring some kind of closure to each one, like they were ghetto detectives or something. But having been in the streets and indulging in the high-stakes dope game for so long, they always knew death was never far off. It was always waiting in the cut for the perfect time to close the curtains on whoever's show was next.

This situation was no different, no matter how close to home it hit. They had to punch the clock. Had work to do. And even though they weren't licensed investigators by any means, they were resourceful, and persuasive as hell.

Especially when they wanted answers.

They knew how to use people's addictions, flaws, and afflictions against them to get exactly what they needed.

Not long after they left Booker's spot, they ended up back at their own trap house and went right back to doing what they were doing before they got that call in the first place.

Pulling the duffel bags out from upstairs, Tony and Mike started laying out everything they'd grabbed from Randy's.

That's when they discovered the tip of the iceberg, and exactly what they'd been looking for this whole time:

Leverage.

Aside from the seven firearms they found, none of which was the specific one they were looking for, they started spreading out all the papers Mike had pulled from the attic onto the table nearby. And that's when they noticed... there were pictures mixed in.

They took a closer look, going through everything one article at a time, and neither of them could believe what they were seeing. As it started to come together, piece by piece, everything became clear.

They analyzed the files, rearranged everything, trying to make sense of it all. And that's when the truth hit them.

They figured out exactly what had happened to Randy, and more importantly, why.

Turns out Randy's military days were anything but typical. In fact, they were a whole lot more elaborate than what anyone had been led to believe. And on top of that, his side hustles, especially selling guns, played a major role in his death.

After going through everything, they discovered who he'd really been involved with. That explained the stacks of cash they'd found too.

But what stood out most were the familiar faces in some of the photographs, pictures that looked like they'd been part of a personal surveillance operation Randy had conducted himself. Probably as a way to keep leverage over the people he was working with.

In those photographs were all kinds of info, faces, documents, details, about Montel Williams, a.k.a. Booker, and two other unknown associates whose names they hadn't recognized until now: Oliver Maxwell and Phillip Andrews...

After being cleared of any wrongdoing in the shooting at his house, once the cops finally arrived and discovered he was one of their own, Oliver Maxwell spared no expense.

He installed cameras all around his home in case those same unknown visitors ever came back. Then, after fixing everything that had been destroyed, he got right back to work plotting, planning, and strategizing how best to conduct surveillance on the two individuals he'd been assigned to watch.

He took the job seriously. Not just to ease his longtime friend's mind, but also to ensure operations could continue without interruptions, so long as the guys on the team could still be trusted. The ones who made *him* and all his partners rich.

And even though he had a known weakness for underage girls, his work ethic and dedication had always set him apart. That's why he and his circle had been able to operate so successfully for so long without interference.

But everything that glitters ain't gold.

And when you can't tell the difference, there's always a cost. No sacrifice, no reward, that was his motto. And it's why Booker never had a real family. Why he couldn't walk away from a lifestyle that slowly ate away at his peace of mind, and eventually, his soul.

He never had the time or opportunity to find real love. Never brought kids into the world. The life consumed him, day in and day out.

And while he might not have wanted for *anything*, his soul craved everything that money couldn't buy, and that no amount of money could replace.

Heading out to do surveillance, Oliver Maxwell decided to take his deceased wife's car, her seven-series BMW. He'd bought it for her as an anniversary gift… the last anniversary they ever got to spend together.

He locked up, then hit the road, headed to the first location Booker had given him. Said it was a place where Tony and Mike could usually be found.

He arrived not long after, and while he didn't see Tony's car, he knew the spot had a garage attached. So, he parked a short distance away and waited, just to see if anyone came or went. Watched the area for a few hours before considering picking up their trail elsewhere, just to be sure he wasn't missing anything.

As Oliver sat outside one of Tony and Mike's known spots, waiting to see if they were even there, his mind drifted. He started reminiscing, back to his high school days.

Took a trip down memory lane.

Back to the first time he met Montel, now known as Booker.

Felt like yesterday, that fateful afternoon their paths first crossed. Thinking now how far they'd come since that day... a day neither of them would *ever* forget.

It was halfway through his senior year of high school. And being as freakishly large and awkward as he was back then, Oliver didn't have many friends. His social life was a complete disaster.

He wasn't a jock, nor was he getting any rhythm from the ladies due to his lack of confidence and low self-esteem, which made his days at school really rough.

He was always being judged and bullied by people who wished they had his size, but not his sight. Even though his physical stature was intimidating, the bifocals he wore made him look more like Steve Urkel than anything else. Nobody took him seriously.

He'd often find himself the butt of everyone's jokes, whenever some insecure teenager wanted to impress their peers by clowning him, projecting their own issues onto him just to deflect attention away from how uncomfortable *they* were in their own skin. They poked fun at how he looked just to feel accepted.

Oliver didn't understand all this at the time, which made them even more successful in tearing him down. He ended up feeling ashamed of his appearance, hiding out in restrooms during passing periods just to avoid the crowds that gathered to egg on the next kid with a set of rehearsed jokes aimed at him.

People would laugh, point, and stare when he walked by, trying to build up their own self-worth by tearing him down.

One day, as Oliver made his way to the restroom during passing period, he noticed a group of guys in there already. That was unusual, most students were rushing to get to class to avoid being late or getting detention.

Then, one of them walked up and snatched the glasses off his face.

Lacking the confidence to defend himself, Oliver just stood there. He'd never really tapped into his physical potential, so he didn't know what he was capable of. He just started whining for the kid to give him his glasses back, as the others joined in, passing them around, trying them on, mocking him. It turned into a game of keep-away.

Then, all of a sudden, he heard a toilet flush, and a stall door swung open.

As the guy came out and saw what was happening, he didn't leave. Didn't join in, either. Instead, he walked right up to the kid who had just put the glasses on his face and *knocked him out cold.*

Before the dude even hit the floor, Booker already had the glasses in hand, and handed them back to Oliver, introducing himself in the process.

From that day forward, the two were like peas in a pod, despite taking completely different paths in life.

And word got around fast about what had happened in that restroom. After that day, nobody ever messed with Oliver Maxwell again. Not only that, but a few girls who had always admired him for his intelligence started showing interest, girls who'd been too ashamed to act on it before, afraid of what people would think.

That's when he met his wife, his high school sweetheart, Roxanne. And the rest was history.

Enlisting in the military fresh out of high school was a whole different story.

The sound of a garage door lifting snapped Oliver out of his flashback. That, and the sudden rev of a car engine brought to life.

Backing out of the garage, in a brand-new Mercedes-Benz, was Tony and Mike.

Now that Oliver had confirmed their location, his work was just beginning.

They pulled out like they were headed somewhere with a purpose, so Oliver started his vehicle and followed at a safe distance, ready to find out exactly where they were going and who he was really dealing with.

Just as he was pulling out of his little hiding spot, his phone buzzed.

He'd gotten a message from his firm; one he'd been waiting on. It was regarding the phone records and financial statements he'd requested on Tony and Mike from their service providers and personal banking institutions.

And just from a quick glance, he saw something interesting, payments had been made for something, or to someone, for reasons that had yet to be determined.

He'd have to investigate that further when the time came.

Even though Oliver had access to all kinds of databases, he still had to run everything through his firm in order to legitimize its use. Otherwise, he could face consequences, possibly lose his licenses, or even do time for constitutional violations.

So, he always had to move accordingly while playing this dangerous game.

But the first thing he needed to know was where these two were going, and then… why…

CHAPTER 11

Riding silently in the car for about fifteen minutes, Tay was the first to break the awkward mute by addressing the elephant in the room.

"Look, man, what happened back there," Tay started to say, but before he could even finish his sentence, Miteous interrupted.

"I already know, bro. It never happened," he said, staring intently into Tay's eyes with a look of reassurance, serious as a heart attack.

But this situation ran deeper than that, so Tay interjected again, adding to Miteous's input.

"Not just that, bro. I know I can trust you, and you always got my back, no doubt. I ain't never questioned yo loyalty, my nigga. But if this shit ever catches up with us, I'm taking it. Period. That shit ain't on you, bro. It ain't yo burden to bear. And I just wantchu to know that, from the heart, bro. Now we don't gotta speak of it again. And I'm keepin' the gun. That's final too," Tay said, returning the same gaze of seriousness that told Miteous not to challenge him on this anymore. His mind was made up.

Miteous started to contest this, then decided not to, slowly nodding his head in agreement. That meant he respected Tay's mind on the matter, and he left it alone.

Then Tay turned up the radio and drove the rest of the way to Grannie's house in silence.

When they finally arrived at their destination, they were about to pull into the driveway to shorten the distance they'd have to walk with all the stuff they were about to go in and stash, when they noticed a car had already been parked there.

Not knowing if somebody was trying to double back on their loot, or if it was the actual homeowner coming to check on the house, they just parked a little ways away so they could see who came out and got in the vehicle, making sure whoever it was wasn't about to come out with their stuff too. That was their main concern at this point.

Posted up for about ten minutes, they noticed a bald-headed white dude finally come out the front door of the house empty-handed, hop in his car, and drive off in the opposite direction.

Facing the harsh reality that their stash house was now compromised, Tay got out the car and told Miteous to sit tight while he went in and attempted to retrieve everything they'd stashed there, so they could just take it somewhere else. Keeping it there only exposed them to a major loss if it got discovered, especially by someone they didn't have any control over. Keeping away from a place that wasn't theirs to begin with...

After retrieving everything he'd stashed, and not wanting to keep trying his luck with abandoned homes, Tay decided to use Ebony's spot for the time being, since that was where he'd been spending most of his time anyway.

But first, he took Miteous to his girlfriend's house, after repeatedly telling him to drill it in her that he had been with her the entire time, solidifying himself an alibi.

Afterward, he arrived at Ebony's a short while later, pulling up to the garage at first and going inside. He was glad to hear the water running, which meant she was in the shower, so he went and lifted the garage and stashed his stuff real quick, stuff he'd been persistently accumulating in the streets for a while. He hid everything as discreetly as he could.

Then, once he unloaded everything, he went back outside to park his hot wheels around the way, as usual, not wanting to bring any unwanted attention to Ebony's spot. This was the type of discretion he operated with his whole criminal career. And even though it was physically and mentally exhausting, it was financially rewarding, which he was all about.

When he finally got back inside the second time, Ebony was out the shower and began asking questions, just out of curiosity.

"Hey babe, didn't I just hear you come in a minute ago when I was in the shower?" she said, just making sure she wasn't hearing things.

But Tay, still on edge and high alert from earlier, started lying off the rip.

"Yea, but I ain't realize I left my phone in the car, and I went back out to go get it. Never know what might happen with 'em after I walk away," he said, referring to his stolen vehicles, trying to divert her attention from the real reason he came and went.

"Aw okay… well, how did things go with Alibimac?" she said in a casual tone, hoping he'd come up on some drugs she could get high off of real quick.

But Tay was so paranoid, he'd forgotten she was the one who introduced them and told him about the meetup the night before.

"Koo. Everything good. Why did he say somethin'? What did you hear? And who you been talkin' to?" he said with a hint of nervousness in his voice he wasn't sure she picked up on or not.

"Nobody and nothin'. Damn, what gotchu buggin'? I was just' makin' sure you was straight, that's all. I told you ya girl was gon' hook you up, didn't I?" she replied, picking up on his awkward vibe, not knowing if it was because he didn't want her in his business anymore. So, she smoothed things over in an attempt to subliminally let him know she'd stuck to her end of the deal. Now it was his turn to do the same, by looking out for her and feeding her drug habit.

But Tay, paranoid and trying to keep his cards close to his chest, changed the subject and the narrative of the conversation.

Noticing her in the mirror pinning up her hair and putting on lotion, he started hinting at sex, trying to get her in the mood. He got overly affectionate, telling her how good she was looking, walking up to her, caressing her shoulder and feeling on her butt.

That made her forget all about her drug habit, and they started messing around right there in the bathroom, which led to the bedroom.

Then, once Ebony fell asleep, Tay left, calling up Patrese on his way out the door…

Tony and Mike made their way to the south side of the city to go hold down Alibimac's trap in an attempt to deal with his regulars, just to see what they had to say.

They were only focused on figuring out who killed their friend, and how to use what they'd found at Randy's to their advantage. They hadn't even noticed they were being tailed.

Going over their conspiracy, brainstorming ideas in the car ride there, Tony was first to share his theory on what he thought was really going on, and what ultimately led to Randy being killed.

"Even though we can't say for certain, I think somebody that was in the military with Randy double-crossed him, bro. And that's where all this shit steamed from. And after all we saw, we know exactly who it was… but why is what we still gotta find out," he said, hoping Mike would add what he was thinking to the equation too.

"Right, and with everything there has been about those overseas routes and ports, it had definitely had somethin' to do with' drugs and trafficking, shit too that happened during them fools' army days, for a fact," Mike added, with emphasis on the word *fact*, agreeing with Tony.

That's when Mike remembered that he'd known a guy who used to frequent Randy's every so often. He told him it was an old army buddy of his who stayed in his apartment building too.

"Ay, I just thought about this dude Melvin my cousin would have over for drinks sometimes, stayed in his building. He said he was in the army with him. You wanna go check him out too when we come from Alibimac's spot?" Mike said excitedly, much happier he was able to remember that than the actual lead itself he'd come up with sporadically.

Making their way to Alibimac's trap, they went inside and posted up with about an ounce of dope, readying themselves for the daily traffic which was surely coming. Both men were in their own thoughts, thinking about the entirety of the situation at hand, when their first customer arrived, demanding a payday's worth. Nicknamed *PayDay* for that very reason.

And when PayDay saw it wasn't Alibimac that opened the hatch of the trap's door, he demanded to know why, immediately.

Once he heard the news, he became increasingly frustrated. Not just because there was a change in business dealings, but because he had just warned Alibimac about not dealing with everybody, especially the young cat he had working the trap for him.

The main reason being that he didn't look out for him the way Alibimac had taught him, trying to preserve his pack. And he'd heard the boy was Rasheeda's son through the grapevine. He'd known Tay's moms since back in the day and knew she wasn't shit, and just figured the apple didn't fall far from the tree.

Moreover, being who he was, PayDay never held his tongue for anybody, especially when he got mad.

"Uh-huh... and I ain't seen that little punk he'd have over here with' him since then either, now that I'm thinkin' 'bout it.

Yaw know who I'm talkin' 'bout?" PayDay said, sliding his money in to get the dope out.

"Nuh-uh, old skoo… who you talkin' 'bout?" Mike replied, standing at the hatch, waiting to hear this last part before he slid the dope out.

"Rasheeda's son," he said, hoping to jog his memory since he didn't really know him by name.

"Rasheeda… Rasheeda… why that sound so familiar?" Mike said, thinking out loud.

"Man, yaw know Rasheeda and Ebony from back in the day, used to do all that stealin' and schemin' shit," PayDay replied, like he just knew they knew exactly who he was talking about.

Then Tony chimed in, "Yea, yea, from over there in the projects, that's right. Shit, it's been a minute since we been down that way. But whatchu say 'bout her son bein' over here?" he said, making sure he heard right.

"Shorty was holdin' down the spot and everything. But I ain't seen him in a few days either," PayDay said, retrieving the dope he paid for and starting to walk off, to go get high as a kite.

By the time Tay made it to Patrese's house, it was late, and her mother had already gone to work. Once she squared things away with all her siblings, her and Tay basically had the place to themselves.

And even though the streets had him numb, he was definitely growing stronger feelings for Patrese, thinking that the feelings were mutual.

"So, what's up, babe? You gon' come stay with' me when I get my own place?" Tay said, laying in Patrese's bed with her while she was acting like her attention was on the television in her room.

"Yea... that's if you ever get yo own place. And we might not even be together then," she said, looking for reassurance that he really planned on being with her.

"Naw, it's not *if*, it's *when*. Shit, it ain't gon' be long now, watch. And girl, watchu talkin' 'bout, you mines, and we definitely gon' brock in," he said reassuringly.

"Yeah, right. You prolly say that to all the girls. You know I'm always hearin' them talkin' 'bout chu," she replied, still playing her little game.

"Man, ain't it nobody worried 'bout them other bitches. I only want chu," he said, more serious this time, causing Patrese to get emotional as well.

Then he said, "I got somethin' for you too," automatically pulling out a six-inch long jewelry box and handing it to Patrese.

Tay said, "Go 'head and open it."

And when she did, she saw inside was a diamond-encrusted tennis bracelet that was at least worth a couple thousand dollars.

"Wow... it's beautiful, babe. Thank you. This is the most thoughtful thing anyone has ever done for me. Now let me give *you* somethin'," she said, as she set her gift on the nightstand and began to start undressing.

Getting down to her panties and bra, she said to Tay, "And I didn't have time to wrap it either."

Then she got on top of him and started kissing him, making her way down to the bulge in his pants, and started giving him the best head he ever had...

Receiving this new information from PayDay had Tony and Mike skeptical. It was odd that one of Alibimac's regulars hadn't seen him, or the youngster he had working for him, after his death, but had seen both of them regularly *before*.

And it was definitely something worth looking deeper into.

But first, they wanted to go by Melvin's after they had wrapped things up there, to see if they could find out what he knew about Randy's military dealings.

Working the trap until night fell, Tony and Mike left with a lot of unanswered questions, and their work cut out for them, as they headed to Melvin's, hoping to get some of them answered at their next destination.

Finally arriving at the Towers apartment complex, Mike got out and told Tony to sit this one out, not wanting to make Melvin feel uncomfortable showing up confronting him about this situation with a complete stranger, having barely known the man himself.

Entering the building alone this time, not knowing where Melvin even stayed exactly, he decided to go to the concierge to see if he could get him to volunteer this information unknowingly.

Being the master manipulator that he was, Mike eventually tricked him into telling him which apartment belonged to

Melvin with no problem. Then he quickly made his way to the correct floor it was located on.

After getting off the elevator and wandering the apartment's hallways a short distance later, he arrived at Melvin's door, knocking on it with a sense of familiarity once he got there. He felt like he was having déjà vu, having just been there before going to see his cousin a dozen times in the past.

He got past the eeriness when Melvin finally answered the door.

"Hey Mike, what's goin' man? Nice to see you. I thought chu might be stoppin' by, havin' heard the news about Randy's passing and everything. My condolences, bro, you know me and Randy went way back. Come on in," Melvin said, stepping aside, welcoming Mike into his home.

Melvin wasn't very tall, but he had long arms and broad shoulders that were bulky, giving him the appearance of a much bigger man. He was light-skinned and talked very fast, with a Southern drawl that covered up his speech impediment, something he had as a result of a head injury from the war.

"Yeah, that's what I was hopin' to talk to you about," Mike said as he entered Melvin's apartment, taking a seat on the living room couch.

Exhibiting his Southern hospitality, Melvin went into the kitchen and grabbed a couple beers from the refrigerator, handing one to Mike once he returned. Then he took a seat on the couch across from him.

"Well, what's on ya mind, man? You know Randy was like family," Melvin said, giving Mike his full and undivided attention.

"I ain't told nobody else this, but me and my day one homeboy are the ones who first discovered Randy in his final state. And I'm the one who called it in, after we cleaned the place up a bit before the cops came. But before I left, I found a lot of interesting things from his military past I hadn't known about. Could've possibly led to his death. I was hopin' you knew more about it, so you could fill in a couple blanks for me... seein' as how you two came up in the ranks together and everything," Mike replied, stopping at this last sentence to gauge Melvin's comfort level on the topic at hand.

"I tell you what, my brotha, you let me know what type of interesting things we talkin' 'bout here, and I'll let chu know what I know about 'em," Melvin said, trained not to give out information freely but still keeping it casual.

"Alrighty then... I found these surveillance photos that included maps and port routes through overseas jungles. And in the pictures were young girls in cages, trucks with lots of drug packages, and crates of guns. There were also three files. One of the files contained information on an Oliver Maxwell... the other on a Phillip Andrews... and the third, a Montel Williams. Does any of this mean anything to you?" Mike said, laying his cards out on the table as he waited, listening intently for a response.

He started noticing how uncomfortable the names and information made Melvin, causing a complete shift in his once candid demeanor right after he'd said all that.

"Ah yes... I'm afraid so. But I had no idea that he'd been personally involved with any of them over here in the States.

That Oliver character was one mean son of a bitch back then, promoted to platoon leader for that very reason. He and Phillip, another high-ranked general, were rumored to have been business partners and made millions using their men to control those ports, sex trafficking young girls, smuggling heroin and guns into the U.S.

"But none of it was ever proven nor formally investigated because nobody was stupid enough to go against those guys, for reasons I'm sure you could imagine. But that last name you said, I've never heard of him. Definitely wasn't enlisted like the rest of us.

"For Randy to have kept evidence of any of that… that was definitely a death warrant. Signed, sealed, and delivered by the Grim Reaper himself. Because although he may have thought nobody knew… these guys got eyes *everywhere*.

"And if you're in possession of this information now, you'd better be careful of your every move too. 'Cause after the military, most of those guys at the top went into different branches of law enforcement, ensuring complete power and immunity over here in the States. For reasons I'm sure you now can imagine," Melvin said with a lot of moxie, taking a sip of his beer and a look of fear in his eyes as he waited to see what else Mike knew about his old friend's dealings.

Now that Mike knew what was at stake, he knew exactly how high the stakes were, with all the key players that'd been involved.

He no longer felt comfortable volunteering what else he thought or may have known and quickly wrapped things up at Melvin's, not knowing exactly where he stood in all this himself. Thanking him for his time and hospitality, he finished up his beer before he left the apartment.

He made a little more small talk on his way out, just to clear the air. Then he left with a whole new perspective about Randy's death, which now seemed like an apparent cover-up...

While Miteous was enjoying Veronica's company, a part of him became emotionally detached, thinking about everything that had transpired in the last forty-eight hours.

He couldn't escape this feeling of a dark cloud that was just developing overhead, in the midst of his being. It had attached itself to him and was now following him around from what had been happening in the streets he'd become involved in.

Not knowing what this meant for his future, he became increasingly depressed.

And when Veronica sensed this, she couldn't help but become sympathetic.

"What's wrong, babe? You look like you just came from a funeral or somethin'," she said.

But little did she know... he basically *did*. He just hadn't been placed in his casket yet.

"I don't know... I just been havin' this feeling that somethin' bad is comin' my way, and I don't know what to do," Miteous replied, referring to his bad juju. He felt it in his soul from the negative energy he'd allowed to attach itself to him, energy that the Universe would surely bring right back his way. And nobody could protect him from it.

He remembered his biblical teachings, that we will all reap what we sow, in one way or another.

"Wat gotchu thinkin' like that, Miteous? Watchu done done now?" Veronica said, knowing that he'd been active in the streets, but never really knowing what he was up to when he wasn't around her. He kept those things from her, for plausible deniability.

"Nothin'… I don't even know why I brought it up. Let's just enjoy this time we got together, Vee. But I do gotta question for you," he said, unable to speak on the things that were really weighing heavy on him.

"Whatever, dude. But I'm always here if you do ever wanna talk about it. And you know you can ask me anything," she replied, a little upset he'd been holding back, but still giving him her complete and undivided attention.

"If I ever got locked up…, would you hold me down?" he said, knowing what her response would be in the moment, but also knowing it was a question only *time* would reveal.

"Of course, babe. I love you. I would do anything for you, dude. But where is all this comin' from?" she said, from the heart, with much moxie.

"I love you too… and I wanted you to be my ride or die since I first laid eyes on you," he replied, not even knowing what a girlfriend was back then, but knowing he wanted something special with Veronica. He ignored her question completely.

Then they held each other close, affectionately, present in the moment as they watched a love story on TV and hung out until it was time for Miteous to go home, feeling passionately inseparable about one another, as time and everything else disappeared out of mind…

Like they were suspended in thin air, as if they were the last two people on Earth…

CHAPTER 12

A couple weeks had passed, and everything seemed like it had returned to normal for Miteous and Tay.

They kept reporting to Booker, pulling off capers and doing odd jobs, bringing him high-quality merchandise to fence. For that, he'd gladly lace their pockets and send them back out on the prowl to do it all over again. The steady flow of money gave them the freedom to enjoy themselves, taking women out on dates and trying to live their best lives.

Tay was even able to get Ebony to cosign on an apartment for him. He had his own place now, which he turned into a mini trap-slash-bachelor pad.

Miteous, on the other hand, finished out the football season on top of his game, getting all kinds of letters from different colleges. The recruiters made it clear they'd be watching and were interested in bringing him on to play once he graduated.

Nobody even mentioned their names in the streets about what happened to Alibimac, or so they thought. Miteous wasn't worried anymore. Neither was Tay.

But the calmest part of a hurricane is always right at the center of it.

And during those couple weeks that had passed, they had no idea about the real waves that were headed their way. They were too busy enjoying the fruits of their labor. By the time the aftermath came knocking, they didn't even see it coming.

It only took Tony and Mike a few days to finally catch up with Ebony, and even less time than that to find out exactly what she knew. When they did, they applied pressure immediately. They didn't know to what extent her role had been, but they felt like she had something to do with their homeboy's death.

Walking home from the store one day, just right around the corner from where she lived, Ebony didn't even realize she was being followed until it was too late.

Dropping the window of the dark-colored sedan, Tony stuck his arm out the door, brandishing a chrome-plated .45.

"Ay bitch, get in the car. And if you run or scream, Imma blow yo ass down, down right here on this sidewalk. So, make the wrong move if you want to."

Not knowing what was going on or what they even wanted with her, and feeling like she'd done nothing wrong, Ebony complied, hoping it was all just a big misunderstanding. She got into the back seat of the Mercedes-Benz, and they drove off.

Once in the car, Ebony started asking questions.

"Whatchu want with me? I ain't done shit to y'all. Hell, I ain't even seen y'all down here in a few years," she said, trying to figure out what was really going on.

Seeing her genuinely fearful for her life and clearly confused, they could tell she hadn't set Alibimac up. But they still believed she had useful information they could use.

"It ain't even you. We came down here to see where yo homegirl or her son at," Mike said, getting straight to the point. He wanted to see how involved she really was because if she gave the information up freely, she was probably innocent. But if she didn't, it meant she knew something. And in his eyes, why protect them unless she was really protecting herself?

Knowing how disloyal drug addicts could be, he pressed her.

"Who, Reesheda? I ain't seen her in a couple days, but she usually be down there off Paxton. And whatchu want with her son? He ain't even old enough to drink yet," she said defensively.

Sensing her protectiveness, Mike lit into her right away.

"Bitch, I'm askin' the fuckin' questions here, aight? And if you don't keep answerin' 'em, them detectives gon' have some of they own when they find yo ass floatin' down Carter Lake. And just 'cause he can't buy a drink don't mean he can't squeeze a trigger," he replied aggressively, upset, revealing what they wanted with her son without even saying it directly.

When he said that last part, her whole vibe changed.

She couldn't believe what she was hearing. She didn't know exactly what happened, but now it was clear, *something* had gone down. It explained everything.

And unless she separated herself from it all, she was about to find herself caught dead in the middle… literally.

"Pull a trigger? Wait… did somethin' happen to Alibimac?" she said, visibly shaken. She already knew what she had to do now, if she was gonna save her own ass from being killed by them, which she knew they wouldn't hesitate to do.

But if she was gonna do it… she was at least gonna make it worth her while.

Following Tony and Mike for about a week, tracking leads and tracing paper trails and phone records they'd unknowingly left behind, Oliver Maxwell was able to determine that their trip to county jail had been everything *but casual*.

He matched up times and dates with money transactions and made note of it all in the preliminary report he gave to Booker.

He even found out who they talked to, though he didn't know the full content of the conversations. Still, he could speculate. And his theories were usually pretty accurate.

But that wasn't how he worked. He only moved off *facts*.

Then he determined what their next move would be. Based on the problems they were now faced with, and from everything he thought they'd been up to, he was able to think a couple steps ahead. So, everything they did, or were about to do, only brought them closer to their own checkmate.

It was all going according to his plan, whether they realized it or not. And *that's* what you paid for when hiring Oliver's Private Investigations to be at your service.

Meeting up with Booker at his shop the following week, Oliver filled him in on everything he'd uncovered.

He waited to see what Booker wanted done about it. Wasn't surprised when it aligned perfectly with what he'd already set in motion.

But even with all the meticulous planning in the world, one still had to account for the plan *not* going accordingly. That's called margin for error.

So, Oliver had a contingency plan in place, just in case.

That was particularly necessary in this instance because Oliver was looking to get rid of *two birds with one stone*. Once he saw what was about to go down as a result of Alibimac's death, the very situation Booker had tipped him off about, and gathered his own intel, he just sat back and let fate take its course.

And even though it wasn't *technically* fate anymore once he intervened, to all parties involved, it wasn't going to feel any different.

Because the end was near for all those that death had it out for.

Like the final destination, it was completely unavoidable.

One Friday afternoon, right before school let out, Patrese had gotten word from a close friend that there was gonna be a big pajama party at a mutual friend's house. The friend asked if she'd be attending.

Not wanting to waste one of the only days of the week she didn't have to sit at home and babysit her siblings, since it was one of her mom's rare days off, Patrese told her friend she'd go. And she got the green light to invite whoever she wanted.

Before she went home that day, she let Tay know what she wanted to do, and that she wanted him to come too. She told him to bring a plus-one, so she could invite her best friend, and they could all hook up afterward at his place for a nightcap.

Tay liked the sound of her plans, especially the part that involved him and Miteous gettin' laid afterward.

He agreed, and they set it all in motion.

Excited about having the girls over to his spot for the first time, Tay couldn't wait to tell Miteous all about it, wanted to see if he was down to have a good time too.

He'd been feeling like everything was going his way lately and was really feeling himself now. He'd completely forgotten about the heat from the Alibimac situation, not even thinking about keeping a low profile while things died down.

When Patrese told him she'd meet them there, he just figured her mom was dropping her and her friend off or something. Thought she was tryna play things off with her home front like always. But little did he know, she was planning on having Booker take her to the mall to shop for some pajamas to wear to the party and then getting a ride from him there.

Once Patrese got home, she called him up. Booker came and got her and her best friend, Chealsey, who she'd told him was her uncle, and they all went shopping.

Booker picked the girls up and took them to the mall. He wasn't really paying attention to them at first, but once he *did*, he instantly got infuriated.

Already insecure around much younger girls, it only made things worse. He couldn't shake the feeling that if it hadn't been for his money and what he brought to the table, they wouldn't have even been entertaining him in the first place.

He kept noticing Patrese checking her phone, then her friend doing the same. Then both of them started laughing and having private conversations that didn't include him.

It pissed him off.

But not wanting to show them how triggered he was, he just kept quiet, staring out the window with a mean mug on his face.

When they got to the mall and Chealsey got out the car, Booker did something that caught Patrese completely off guard, something that made her regret ever getting involved with this older man, especially now that she'd fallen head over heels for Tay.

Right before Patrese was about to open her door and get out the car too, Booker grabbed her by the wrist, tight as a vice grip, with an aggression she'd never seen from him before. He stared at her cold.

"Where the fuck did you get this at? And don't lie to me either, Pat, 'cause I'm gon' find out," he said, giving her a look that could kill.

"It was a gift. And let go of me, nigga, is you crazy?" she snapped, referring to the diamond bracelet she was wearing on her left wrist.

"A gift? A gift from who? Did your *uncle* give you this?" he asked, letting go of his grip.

Not wanting to expose her other relationship and have to deal with his reaction, especially in front of her friend, she just nodded yes.

He looked satisfied with that answer.

Then they both got out the car like nothing ever happened and entered the mall.

Even though Chealsey had heard the whole conversation and seen what just went down, she didn't say anything. She wasn't blind to the fact that this older man wasn't *really* related to Patrese. But not wanting to get on her friend's bad side by stepping into her business, she just kept a mental note and stayed vigilant from that point on.

Staring out the window, Patrese felt guilty for betraying Tay. She'd given Tony and Mike information that cleared her name in that whole Alibimac situation a few weeks ago, and she'd been thinking of a way to tell Tay what was going on.

But she couldn't work up the courage to do it.

She kept getting this gut feeling that something bad was going to happen to him because of what she did. She finally decided to give him a call, to come clean about what she'd done, just so he could at least have a fighting chance to be prepared for what was coming.

After all, it wasn't *her* actions that actually caused his death. And if he'd told her what *he'd* done, then she wouldn't have been blind to the truth either.

Getting rolled up on, guns drawn on her, interrogated, when all she was trying to do was help his ass out, she still felt like she had to make it right by letting him know.

Grabbing her phone, she dialed up his number right away.

But Tay didn't answer the first time.

She tried again. When it went straight to voicemail the second time, she figured his phone died. She decided to give him a few hours before trying again.

Assumed maybe he just wanted some space or was busy hustling, which had often been the case lately, now that he had his own place.

She understood the kind of independence he was after. And she'd been happy to help him get there.

Not knowing what else to do, she just left him a message, told him to return her call *immediately* because it was something important.

She knew how important it was for someone to grow on their own, especially him. She'd grown up best friends with his mother and had seen firsthand how that woman had always put her own selfish desires and bad habits before motherhood. She used Tay to get what she wanted every single time.

So Patrese let him be… hoping she wasn't too late to warn him…

CHAPTER 13

A Pajama Jammy Jam.

"Hell yea, I'm down, bro! That sound like a nice time, come and get me ASAP. Mom dukes and 'em been gettin' on my nerves anyways, always arguin'. I can't wait to get outta here. And bring some of that good shit too, not none of that backyard boogie you be slangin' to them niggas in yo complex either," Miteous said, laughing, having just gotten word from Tay about the big-time party he'd been invited to.

"Aight bro, I gotchu. And what chu talkin' bout foo, you know all I got is that good shit. I'll be there in like fifteen minutes, so be ready," Tay replied, getting off the phone with Miteous and heading to get dressed.

He checked his stash spot before he did and saw he was down to his last couple ounces of hydroponic kind bud. He set some aside for him and Miteous for later, having already sold off all the powder he came up on after the Alibimac situation. His pockets were just as full as his refrigerator.

After Tay got dressed and checked himself out in the full-body mirror in his room, he realized he'd almost forgotten to bring out the pair of $2,000 matching chains he bought personalized at the mall last week. They were for him and Miteous, a surprise he planned to hit him with before the party.

They were all 24-carat gold plated, diamond-encrusted, with the initials MBK on them, *My Brother's Keeper*, symbolic of everything they'd been through together. A token of love and loyalty for the friend that had become a brother to him over time. Tay thought it was a nice touch and felt like they deserved to stunt a little bit. *What's the point of getting money if nobody sees it?* That was his mentality, especially coming from nothing.

Looking around his place like he was seeing it for the first time, he knew it could use some organizing but still felt a sense of accomplishment having manifested this humble abode. He couldn't wait to see where his grind took him next.

Exiting the apartment, one he planned on cleaning up later or having his girl do it for him, he figured he still had time for all that. He was in such a rush to go get Miteous that he didn't even realize he'd forgotten to charge his phone, which died shortly after he hung up. But he didn't forget to bring his gun or where he parked the car he'd stolen earlier just for the occasion.

Staying a few blocks away from a gas station had its perks, especially for Tay, who'd been plotting on some nicer wheels to pull up to the party scene with. When a brand-new Dodge Charger pulled up to the pumps with the music blasting, trying to draw everybody's attention, the owner had no idea he'd drawn the *wrong* attention.

As soon as the man went inside to pay for gas, Tay, who'd been posted on the side of the building watching from the shadows, saw his opportunity. Casually walked over to the car, hopped in, and drove off like it'd been his the whole time. He gassed it up, parked it around the corner from his complex, and was now just waiting on Miteous.

What he hadn't noticed, though, was the dark-colored sedan that had been watching him in the parking lot the whole time, occupied by two adversaries he didn't even know he had.

"Look bro, there that lil nigga go right there. How you wanna handle this?" Mike asked Tony as soon as they spotted the young man that fit the exact physical description Ebony had given them. She'd even told them where to find him.

"We gon' wait. Let's just see where he go, too many cameras and witnesses around here, and all it take is one if they hear the shots. Just be patient. We gon' get him," Tony replied with the calmness and focus of someone who'd done this plenty of times before.

"Yea you right. And plus, didn't Ebony say this nigga ain't even got a car?" Mike said, trying to remember the avalanche of info she'd dumped on them after they'd threatened to kill her, then gave her some dope once she became cooperative.

"Uh huh. But she also said this lil nigga done stole enough cars to fill a dealership lot too, so let's see how long he stay on foot and where he go. I got somethin' for his ass, watch," Tony said, squinting his eyes menacingly, never taking them off Tay, letting Mike know he had it all planned out.

A few blocks away from the complex, they were about to hop out and run up on him, until they saw Tay hop in a new Dodge Charger and take off. That forced them to follow from a safe distance and wait for another opportunity.

When Miteous finished getting dressed and made sure all his responsibilities were taken care of, Tay had pulled up to come scoop him for the party.

Once he got outside after hearing the horn honk a couple times, he almost overlooked the ride, being so used to Tay pulling up in old raggedy cars. He barely even noticed the brand-new Charger parked down the street. But once he did, his whole vibe changed, and he started feeling himself too.

Hopping in the passenger seat, turned up for the night ahead, he couldn't help but start clowning Tay immediately.

"Man, this what I'm talkin' 'bout bro, go big or stay home, my nigga. 'Bout time you start jackin' somethin' worth takin'. I was startin' to think of you as the junkyard version of *Grand Theft Auto*," Miteous said, laughing excessively.

"Them other people prolly wanted you to drive off with they shit, tired of lookin' at 'em they damn self," he added, still jokin' on the quality of Tay's previous rides.

"Yea whatever bro, I get it how I live. Caught this fool slippin' the other day, came up on this whip just for us tonight. And guess what else, bro…" Tay said, looking at Miteous like he was a contestant on *The Price is Right*, waiting on him to guess.

"Wassup bro? What else you got up yo sleeve?" Miteous replied, letting the dramatic pause linger like Tay wanted.

"Patrese bringing her fine ass homegirl with her by the crib tonight too. She told me she just broke up with her boyfriend, lil thick ass Chealsey, and you know what that mean…" Tay said, smiling at Miteous and throwing out a hand for the dap.

Miteous shook him up enthusiastically, but before he could say anything, Tay added, "And look under yo seat, bro. That's for you too."

When Miteous reached under and pulled out the chain, he was at a loss for words. Tay untucked his to show they were a matching set. Miteous hurried up and threw his on, checking himself out in the mirror, and just kept thanking Tay over and over.

Then Tay drove off, burning rubber all the way down the street with the music turned all the way up...

Coming from the mall after dropping the girls off at their destination, Booker hadn't even noticed the unusual amount of traffic forming out front of the residence he'd just pulled away from.

He'd only been told it was an all-girls slumber party, something Patrese made up to hide her hand and ease his mind. He'd been angry ever since officially confirming it was Tony and Mike who robbed him and had someone else killed to cover up their wrongdoing.

Now they were possibly in possession of the gun that could crumble his whole operation, one that wasn't just a family heirloom but held secrets from his checkered past that he *could not* afford ending up in the wrong hands.

He was starting to feel like his luck had finally run out. Completely overwhelmed by the whole situation, Booker couldn't shake the weight of what was coming.

Back in the day, he'd killed a man named Mark Andrews, the one who ran the heroin game before him. That move paved his way to the top, letting him step into the role and secure his overseas plug.

He started as a corner boy, worked his way all the way up, and when the opportunity presented itself, he took it.

Then he took out two more of his top lieutenants who'd refused to jump ship once he implemented a new order of business and established his takeover. He kept the gun as a souvenir, ironically, as a reminder to himself to never trust anyone or get caught slipping during his reign of terror.

But now, it felt like a cancerous curse he wished he'd gotten rid of a long time ago. One that had now become a detriment to him.

Finding himself in this position because of the people he brought around was something he was never prepared to deal with. But if this was the beginning of his end, if this was how the game was about to flip on him, then he was gonna make sure he wasn't the only one getting checkmated for putting the wrong pieces on the board. That was for damn sure.

Caught up in his own murderous thoughts, he was just about to call Oliver and bake a cake with Tony and Mike being the main ingredients, when he stopped at a red light.

And he couldn't believe his eyes when he looked up and spotted Tony's dark-colored sedan creeping through the neighborhood, headed in the same direction he had just come from. Barely noticing them out his peripheral, he was absolutely positive they hadn't seen him, just like he never saw Oliver.

Smashing the gas, he quickly hit a U-turn as soon as he saw them turn down a backstreet a few blocks away. He hurried up and tried to catch up with them, hoping to catch them slipping real quick and feign surprise whenever anyone brought him the bad news.

But once he reached the street they went down, he was pissed when he got to the end and didn't see their car in sight anymore. Not wanting to blow the opportunity, he just decided to patrol a few more blocks to make sure they weren't around, still remaining optimistic they'd circled back or were hiding somewhere nearby.

Before calling it quits and leaving all the dirty work for his expert to handle, no matter how personal this was now, he continued to circle through the neighborhood just a little while longer...

Miteous and Tay finally arrived at the party, making a grand entrance by doing donuts in the middle of the street, drawing the attention of the many onlookers. The party was jam-packed.

Aside from the cars coming and going, doing drop-offs and pickups, the music was blasting. From outside looking in, it looked like everybody was having a good time.

Miteous was so worried about going in and showing off his new chain and getting his boogie on, he hadn't even realized they'd been followed there.

And Tay was so focused on finding a secure parking spot and linking up with Patrese, he wasn't fully aware of his surroundings like he normally would be.

"Ay bro, go up in there and see if you can find the girls. I'm 'bouta go find a good spot to park this bitch in case the cops show up around here or somethin' later," Tay said, pulling up to the front and letting Miteous out, happy to go make his presence felt at the party.

"Aight then bro, I catchchu on the inside," Miteous replied, getting out.

159

Once he got inside the party, Miteous really started feeling himself, especially when they started playing one of his party favorites, *Sweatin'* by Twista.

He smiled at the girls nearby, dancing and carrying on, greeting everybody he knew. And even though he never drank like that, he had a few cups of the spiked punch they had set out for everyone. It boosted his mood even more.

He was vibing, surrounded by people from every side, when some familiar faces worked their way through the crowd.

"Hey Miteous, where's yo boy at?" Patrese asked, her best friend in tow, glossy-eyed, looking like she'd already found her way to the punch bowl one too many times. She was looking sexy in her brand-new pajamas that looked like they'd never been worn before.

"Awh wassup Patrese, he comin'. He just had to go find somewhere to park; you know how that go. But he sent me in here to find y'all for him though, so he could come straight for you when he do," Miteous replied, making her smile when she heard that last part.

Then he immediately turned his attention to the girl standing next to her and instantly felt drawn to her.

"Yea, that sound like him. But anyways, I almost forgot, this my best friend Chealsey. You prolly seen her around skoo," Patrese said, noticing Miteous staring at her before she introduced them. "And Chealsey, this Tay's best friend, Miteous. Imma let y'all talk and everything, I gotta go pee real quick," she added, scurrying off to the restroom.

"Nice to meetchu officially, Chealsey," Miteous said, embracing her with a friendly hug, eyes clearly filled with interest.

"Because I definitely remember seeing you around before, but I heard you already was boo'd up, so I just fell back, was all," he added, making that last part up. He'd heard about her recent breakup and wanted confirmation she was ready and willing to make a smooth transition.

"Nice to meet you too, and that was past tense. And we'd been having problems for a while, so it was long overdue. But I did come to a couple of your football games this season and saw you playing… you were really good," Chealsey replied, giving him a look of admiration.

"Thanks. I wish I would've known you was watchin'. I would've really showed out," Miteous said flirtatiously, flexing his chest out a little, peacocking.

Chealsey laughed and started blushing. He could tell she was really feeling him now, and the vibe was just right. They kept going back and forth until Chealsey said something that suddenly put Miteous on high alert, making him uncomfortable outta nowhere.

They got on the subject of sex, and Miteous, playfully revealing that they didn't have to move as quickly as Patrese and Tay had, brought up the day he walked in on them after they'd just met. That's when Chealsey spoke on how wild her friend was, and then accidentally hinted at the fact that they might've been dropped off at the party by an older man. She said Patrese claimed it was her uncle, but Chealsey didn't believe that's who he really was.

When Miteous asked why not, Chealsey told him. And once he asked what dude looked like, she gave a physical description that only matched one person Miteous knew perfectly, Booker.

Then outta nowhere, Patrese came back, wanting to know what they'd been talking about. That's when Miteous really started paying attention to her and saw it.

The same tennis bracelet Tay had found that day in the alley was now on Patrese's wrist.

And from the sound of things, this had created a much bigger problem than he or Tay were even prepared to deal with.

Before Miteous could go outside and get to the bottom of everything and figure out the full situation with Tay, he was already coming into the party, with his mind deadset on one thing and one thing only: Patrese.

Heading straight in their direction.

Patrese lit up as soon as she saw Tay, dappered down fresh with his brand-new chain on. She grabbed him by the hand immediately and hit the dance floor after they embraced in a long hug and kiss, showing off the gift he had given her, to him, before they disappeared into the crowd like two long-lost lovers reuniting after years apart.

Miteous, feeling like he had all night to talk to him, put it on hold for now, still thinking about how good he and Chealsey had just hit it off. Noticing her standing alone now, he hurried over to stand by her side just as another one of his songs came on, and took her by the hand to the dance floor too…

Tony and Mike noticed Tay had parked the car a few blocks away from what looked like a party. They could've caught him slipping on his walk back to it, but Tony intervened, putting his own plan in motion, one a lot smoother than that.

He pulled out his phone and called up his longtime mechanic and handyman, who owned his own towing company, to come tow the car. That way, when Tay came to get it, they could just ambush him on foot, and he wouldn't have anywhere else to go but straight to the morgue.

After sitting out there for close to an hour, the tow truck finally showed up. Tony gave the driver a hundred dollars to tow the Charger away and leave it on the side of the road somewhere else.

Then Tony and Mike drove a little ways off to park the car they came in, concealing its identity from any potential witnesses, and proceeded to camp out between some houses that had the perfect view of where the Charger had been parked. That way, when Tay came looking, all he'd find was a full clip of hollow points.

Dressed in all black, with gloves and ski masks, Tony and Mike sat there in the cut, waiting on their prey to come to them this time…

Hitting one more block, which basically brought him right back to the same street he'd dropped the girls off at, if not a block or two over, Booker drove slowly, looking up and down both sides of the street, trying to figure out just where the hell Tony and Mike went that quick.

He was starting to think his mind was playing tricks on him and was about to call it quits and exit the neighborhood he felt like he'd been circling for hours.

He turned down one more backstreet he hadn't hit yet since leaving the first time and finally spotted the dark-colored Mercedes he'd been looking for the whole time and slammed on the brakes.

Not wanting to get overly excited in case he couldn't capitalize off the opportunity inconspicuously, he decided to drive by it casually to take a closer look inside.

But once he rolled up on the car at a slow and steady pace, he discovered nobody was even in the vehicle.

Knowing this wasn't their neck of the woods and they didn't have anybody that stayed over there, he just parallel parked a couple car lengths back and waited a while to see if they'd return, thinking it might've been some female's house they'd been at. He knew how Tony was about his car, so he figured dude had to still be nearby...

As midnight approached, the party came to an end and the music stopped. The host thanked everyone for coming and having a good time, then asked everybody to leave.

Four people they didn't have to say that twice to were Tay, Miteous, Patrese, and Chealsey because they already knew what they were about to do next.

Getting outside the party was when Miteous remembered the conversation he wanted to have with Tay. So instead of falling back and waiting curbside with the ladies while Tay went to go fetch the car, Miteous volunteered to go with him so they could speak in private.

He figured this was probably the last time they'd be alone without the girls hearing what they were talking about.

So, while him and Tay went to go get the car, the girls waited in front of the house with all the other partygoers waiting on their rides too.

Getting to the end of the street, a couple steps behind Tay, Miteous started up the conversation, saying exactly how he felt, still a little tipsy.

"Ay bro... I ain't tryna ruin yo night or yo connection, but how much you even know about ol' girl, for real?" Miteous said, speeding up a little to catch up to Tay.

"Who? Patrese? Shit, prolly as much as she know about me. And why you ask that? Whatchu know about her that I don't is the question," Tay replied, not really worried about what Miteous had to say, still walking at the same pace.

"Man, I think she playin' you, bro. Her best friend told me about some shit in her drunken state at the party, and it sound like to me, they got dropped off by Booker, after he took 'em to the mall and bought her shit," Miteous said, his voice filled with skepticism.

"Booker? What would she be doin' wit that old-ass nigga?" Tay said, damn near stopping in his tracks completely, turning his back to the direction they were headed just to look Miteous in the eyes. They weren't far from where he'd parked the car now.

"I don't know, man... that's what I'm sayin'. Bro, Chealsey said she lied and told her it was her uncle, but said she saw the nigga snatch her by the wrist about that bracelet like a jealous lover, askin' her where she got it from and shit, and did her uncle give it to her?" Miteous replied, looking Tay dead in the eyes, sad he had to be the bearer of bad news.

It surprised Tay and made him laugh a little the way it threw him back to their kindergarten days.

"Man, bro… I ain't trippin' off no female here…"

CHAPTER 14

"Ay remember that bro was the last thing Miteous ever heard Tay say…"

Then Tony and Mike came out of the shadows, firing from afar, walking closer and closer with every shot. When Miteous heard the first shot, he ducked down low before attempting to flee, probably saving his own life with that sudden move. Within the next ten paces he took from where the shooting started, he heard at least three bullets fly past his head.

When he finally got a split second to look back and check on Tay, who had tried to shoot back instead of turning and running like he did, laying down some cover fire for the both of them, he saw him laid out on the pavement, motionless. The reflection from his chain glistened under the moonlight, along with the chrome pistol he died with still in his hand.

After the two gunmen stopped firing and retreated, Miteous came out from hiding behind a parked car along the street and ran up to Tay's body. Once he got close enough to smell the gunpowder mixed with the iron in his blood from the open wounds, he saw him take his last breath. Staring up at him, Tay's eyes looked scared for the first time in his life. Then Tay made one last movement before the energy left his body forever, he reached for his chain, almost like he was trying to tell his best friend goodbye.

It was MBK for life as he let out his last sigh, and a tear came rolling down his cheek.

Right then and there, Miteous Reese made up his mind. He was all in when it came down to being his brother's keeper too because Tay had just saved his life, and he felt like he owed it to him even after death. As long as there was breath in his body, he was going to ride.

If he hadn't made that move without hesitation, he knew without a doubt he'd be laying dead right next to him. So Miteous bent down and began prying the chrome-plated .357 Magnum from Tay's cold, rigid dead hand, discovering it had been fired several times. Only two bullets remained, which meant Tay *did* die firing back, trying to protect them.

Confirming this, Miteous became so overwhelmed with emotion he grabbed the gun and took off running, heading back toward where the party had ended, with murderous intent. Even though the shooters wore masks that concealed their identities, he now had a good idea who they were and exactly what this was all about.

But before he got all the way back to where he was headed, Miteous stopped in his tracks. He started throwing up and crying, thinking about Tay's last words. Tay had asked him if he remembered the same thing he told him back in kindergarten, the story about the girl Miteous had been jealous over that had forged their bond forever. And with everything they'd been through since then, how it all ended was something he was never going to be able to forget…

Jogging back to the car after hitting their target, Tony and Mike were irate. They'd gone into the situation thinking it was going to be simple and easy, since they had the drop. They weren't expecting Tay to return fire, and definitely not expecting Mike to get struck in the leg.

Not knowing if the other youngster they'd seen Tay with had a gun too, they had to retreat. They thought he'd be by himself.

Getting in the car, Tony turned on all the interior lights to assess the damage. Mike discovered a gaping hole in his calf, and the bullet looked like it was still lodged in there.

"Man… is I'm trippin or did that lil niggah have a three-fifty-seven?" Mike said to Tony, wincing from the pain in between shallow breaths.

"I don't know. It was a chrome-plated revolver though, that's for damn sure. Look at that hole, man. You gotta keep pressure on it till we can get it closed up," Tony replied, studying the severity of his friend's wound.

"Ight bro, but no hospitals. You know they ask too many questions. Take me to Shameeks. She's a RN, she'll know how to take care of dis… and you don't think that could have been the same gun, do you?" Mike said, still referring to the chrome revolver he saw.

Tay shot back with… "shit it could be, ain't no tellin'. You know how this street shit go. But I'ma drive by there real quick since you got such a good feeling about,"

"But the cops will be here any minute. You sure you wanna risk it over a hunch?" Tony replied, starting up the car, about to pull off into traffic, waiting for a car to drive by that had been slowly approaching.

But as soon as it reached them, it stopped…

Waiting in his parking spot for over an hour, it was about twenty minutes past midnight and Booker just kept going over every little detail in his head, trying to figure out exactly where he went wrong. That's when he heard multiple gunshots close by.

Startled but not shaken, he started up his vehicle just in case but stayed right where he was. Not even five minutes later, he saw Tony and Mike, dressed in all black and wearing ski masks, come running out from the side of some houses at the end of the street, headed straight for Tony's car. So, he killed his lights.

Watching from a distance, he didn't know what to make of the scene playing out in front of him. But he knew what he came to do, regardless of the unnecessary heat they'd just brought by doing whatever it was they had done.

And whatever it was, by the looks of it, had just gotten one of them shot.

Not knowing exactly what went down, he now knew without a doubt these two had something to do with it. So, it was probably only a matter of time for them anyway.

Pulling slowly out of his parking space and approaching Tony's car from behind, he got confirmation it was them when the interior lights came on. They took their masks off and sat there, going back and forth about something. Then Tony started the engine, which lit up the brake lights.

Booker checked his gun's magazine, making sure he had one in the chamber before pulling all the way up on them. He lowered his window as he drove up smoothly on the driver's side.

And when his vehicle lined up perfectly with Tony's, Tony absentmindedly looked over, like a deer caught in headlights. Completely off guard, he was staring Booker in the face.

And it was only then that he finally noticed... he was also staring down the barrel of Booker's gun.

"Message from Fleewell, muthafuckas!" Booker yelled before firing seventeen from his Glock into the car at both of them, leaving them slumped over full of holes. Then he drove off just as slow and steady as he approached, trying not to draw any more unwanted attention to the scene, besides the gunshots that could be heard throughout the neighborhood.

Booker then proceeded to head back to the shop, even though it was late. He planned on posting up until sunrise, having already agreed to meet with Oliver first thing the next morning. What he didn't know was that Oliver had already been watching the entire time, picking up on his tail as soon as he drove off, after witnessing him kill Tony and Mike...

Miteous finally pulled himself together.

His whole mentality changed just like that. Fueled by rage and hatred, he went from Tony Dorsett to Tony Montana. He knew what had to be done, and he wasn't about to let nothing get in the way of him seeking revenge for Tay.

Walking back to the party a few blocks away, he wasn't even fazed by the gunshots he'd heard in the distance, not far from where he had just come from.

Miteous finally pulled himself together, and his whole mentality changed just like that. Fueled by rage and hatred, he went from Tony Dorsett to Tony Montana, because he knew what had to be done, and wasn't about to let *nothing* get in the way of him seeking revenge for Tay.

Walking back to the party a few blocks away, he wasn't even fazed by the several gunshots he'd heard in the distance, not far from where he had just come from. Even if he was curious to know what it had all been about, he just continued on his quest to get to the bottom of all the unanswered questions he still had.

And he was about to start asking them to the number one person he felt had the most secrets, and told the most lies, leading up to this situation: Patrese Walker.

Once he heard the sirens and saw the lights flickering through the houses as he got closer, he knew he had to be real careful about whatever it was he decided to do. Having been so involved with everything lately and now carrying a murder weapon in the middle of all this, he was well aware of how high the stakes had just become.

But retaliation was a must. And revenge was a dish he planned on serving cold and direct.

Spotting the girls huddled up with a couple others they knew, all waiting on rides too, Miteous locked eyes with Patrese and stormed straight toward her. He was furious. The second he saw her; he demanded a one-on-one conversation.

"Listen, I don't know what the fuck you got goin' on wit deez niggas out here, playin' both sides, but if yo shit just got my best friend killed, I swear to God you gon' regret the day y'all paths crossed. So, now's your only chance to come clean about what the fuck you know… or I'm shortenin' up yo night right here, right now," Miteous said after pulling her to the side, gun in hand, dead serious.

"Wait, what? Tay's dead? You tellin' me that was y'all that was in all that... around the way? Oh my God... no, why?" Patrese replied frantically, breaking down in tears, genuine shock and fear taking over.

But before she could use it as a defense mechanism, Miteous demanded answers.

"Patrese, listen to me, I'm not fuckin' playin' wit cho ass. I know about you and Booker. I know 'bout all that. But what I don't know is, did he know about you and Tay? And what made him trip about that bracelet on yo wrist?"

"And did you tell him who really gave it to you?" Miteous asked, locking eyes with her like he already knew the truth, and even if she told it, it'd only be confirming what he already suspected.

"What... how did you..."

"No, because it wasn't none of his business. And I only told him what he wanted to hear, which was that my uncle gave it to me... 'cause he hustles for him and could afford it. And that way it wouldn't seem like I was sleepin' with someone else to have been given it in the first place," Patrese replied, half answering her own question out loud about how Booker must've found out.

"So, who is your uncle anyway? And why did Booker automatically assume he gave it to you for that? That still don't make sense," Miteous said, sensing she was still leaving something out.

"His name Mike... and he got a partner named Tony who always with him all the time. And they work for Booker too, always doin' all his dirty work. And I don't know... he probably

173

think they done stole it from him or somewhere or somethin', 'cause that's what they do too," Patrese replied, giving up everything she knew. She even started speculating, hoping it'd be enough to calm Miteous down and get the gun off her.

But as soon as she said that last part, Miteous took off running again.

This time, Patrese was yelling after him, asking how they were supposed to get home now, which was the last thing on his mind.

He kept running down the street a few blocks, turning down a backstreet where he could see red, white, and blue lights brightening up the dark, moonlit sky. As he got closer, running down a couple more short blocks, he saw there was a whole *other* crime scene being preserved, not far from where Tay had been laying dead.

And he didn't know what was going on now.

Trying to get a closer look from beyond the yellow tape, he saw it looked like everything had been centered around a vehicle. But once police started canvassing the area, asking people in the crowd what they saw or heard, Miteous was long gone.

He never got to see what had actually happened, officially, or who had occupied the car being investigated.

He just took off on foot, headed toward his next destination: Booker's Pawn Shop…

Booker got to the pawn shop and waited in his car for a while, trying to clear his head of all the mixed emotions he had going on about doing what he felt had to be done. Because even though his actions were justified for the level of betrayal Tony and Mike had demonstrated, they were still like sons to him. He'd brought them up from nothing, and it hurt him deeply to have ended their relationship on those terms.

But business was business.

It wasn't nothing personal about it at the end of the day.

Booker was immediately startled when he heard a tap on his passenger side window. Recognizing who it was, he quickly pressed the unlock button. Oliver Maxwell got into the car.

"Man, you still got it, Bossman. Just when I was thinkin' you'd gone soft on me. You know I seen that whole thing, don't you?" Oliver said, closing the door behind him, referring to the hit he'd just watched Booker pull on his own guys.

"I thought I told you; you could call it quits once the sun went down on yo tail," Booker replied, reiterating their agreement, still not knowing Oliver had been watching.

"Relax man, it's all good. I'm retired now. Ain't got nothin' else to do, with my wife's passing and all... it's more like a hobby for me now, at this point. Seein' all my work through from start to finish. Don't even sweat it," Oliver said, with a menacing undertone Booker didn't pick up on.

"You 'member how we did those Andrews brothers back in the day? The ones that were givin' you problems before I had you take over, don't you?" Oliver continued casually, referring to how he'd set up his own business partner, fellow General of his command, and had Booker kill his main distributor, who was also his little brother, back in the States.

That eliminated their only competition along with his two other most trusted underbosses, giving Oliver Maxwell complete control of the street market. It made him the head of the heroin game, which no one else knew but him.

"How could I forget? You one smooth operator, my friend. I can give you that. Taught me everything I know. But... whatever happened to ol' Phillip anyway?" Booker asked, sounding genuinely concerned now about a potential loose end, even if it wasn't his responsibility initially.

"Ah, well, you know... pretty much the same thing that happens to all dirty government officials who get busted. Got stripped of his rankings and lost in the same system they were once trusted to protect and serve, unfortunately. After doing over twenty years in a federal prison somewhere, I heard he got out on supervised release. Workin' somewhere as a correctional officer or somethin' now," Oliver said like the man was the last of his worries. He had clearly written him off completely as a threat.

To Oliver, the man was under constant watch, stuck on federal papers, and had never even suspected Oliver was the reason he got busted. He probably still thought he was the smartest one in the room.

And even though no one ever questioned Oliver about his war crimes, or the conspiracies overseas that got a bunch of his people locked away and dishonorably discharged, he never left anything to chance.

Now rich beyond his wildest dreams, with complete immunity through the FBI, and Booker as the face of his secure network, the gatekeeper of all his lifelong secrets, Oliver realized he'd only been prolonging the inevitable.

Seeing Booker do what he did… that's when he changed faces on him.

He pulled out his gun.

And by the time Booker realized what the whole awkward exchange had really been about, it was too late.

Oliver Maxwell had the complete drop on him, just like he'd taught him how to do, flawlessly, without fail, throughout all the years of cleaning up liabilities…

CHAPTER 15

"Man, what the fuck you doin'?!" Booker said frantically to Oliver, who now had him at gunpoint.

"Let's go. Out the car. Get inside. This is how it gotta be, my friend," Oliver replied, making it clear he'd not only made up his mind, but had already planned exactly what he was about to do.

"After all I've done for you?! This is the way you repay me, muthafucka?" Booker said, more out of hurt than anger as the bitterness from betrayal slowly started to settle in.

"All you've done for me? Naw, take a look around, Montel. This is all I've done for you. If I hadn't given you the drop on those shipments and forced your hand to level up, you'd still be nickelin' and dimin' it. Content with a crumb like the rest of these lowlifes from Larimore to Midtown. So, spare me from all the charades," Oliver said coldly, the gun still aimed at Booker's center mass as he followed close behind him, unknowingly entering the pawn shop's corridor for the last time.

Once they got inside Booker's office, Oliver motioned for him to sit.

"All I wanna know, man, is... why now? After all this time. Haven't I been loyal?" Booker asked, trying to stall him out while inching toward a pistol he kept nearby, still hoping he could grab it if he moved quickly.

"What goes up must come down. And every good thing must come to an end, my friend. You takin' this way too personal, it's only business," Oliver stated nonchalantly.

Knowing Booker too well, Oliver figured he was gonna go for a gun as a last-ditch effort. So, he raised his arm first and shot him in the stomach.

Booker fell out the chair, gasping for air and clutching his wound. Oliver looked down at him and said:

"Plus, I never liked child molesters anyway."

Then he shot him again, killing him instantly, right there in his own office.

He fired one more time at the front door, shattering the glass before leaving. Then wiped down everything he'd touched, leaving the gun out in plain view, right near the entrance, so whoever walked in next would instinctively pick it up, not knowing it was the murder weapon.

Their prints would be all over it.

After deleting the video footage, Oliver walked out the shop and went to his car, waiting on the last part of his plan to go into effect…

It was now almost two o'clock in the morning, and Miteous had been walking for a couple hours, going over everything in his head. That's when he spotted an old lady come outside, start up her car, and go back into her house, probably getting ready for work.

Looking up at the sky, not knowing if it was Tay watching and helping him along or not, he felt a sudden confidence booster. He decided to take a page out of Tay's playbook. He walked over to the woman's vehicle, hopped in, and took off, headed straight for Booker's.

He cut the time in half and arrived at the pawnshop not long after. Exiting the vehicle, he headed toward the building, ready to confront Booker about the conspiracy he suspected him of being part of, the one that got his best friend killed.

If Booker admitted it, he'd kill him.

If he didn't, he was going to make him give up the drop on Tony and Mike.

Approaching the front of the pawnshop, Miteous got a gut feeling. He heard a voice in his head telling him to turn around. Something didn't feel right. But he was too angry and overwhelmed by emotion.

He pulled the gun out and kept walking.

He couldn't abandon his mission without getting the closure he was after. He ignored every red flag, every voice telling him to leave, and just kept seeing Tay's lifeless body on the pavement, grasping for air, reaching for his MBK chain, the same chain Miteous was wearing right now.

He kept moving forward.

He'd been dismissing those warnings for hours. He was all in. He'd convinced himself this was what he *had* to do, no matter what.

When he finally got to the building, he saw the door was shattered, like someone had gotten to Booker before him or had already broken in. Curious to see what was going on inside, he stepped through the busted glass, hearing it crunch under his shoes as he walked deeper into the pawnshop.

He crept low, moving quiet.

About twenty feet in, heading toward the back corridor where Booker's office was, he spotted a gun on the floor. He picked it up, checked the clip, it was loaded, and smelled like it had just been fired.

That's when he knew he'd made a big mistake…

Oliver Maxwell had parked his vehicle a little ways down the street, like he always did. But this time, it was so he could take up a perfect vantage point. He sat there waiting for the second phase of his plan to begin, Operation: Wet 'Em Up Then Set 'Em Up.

Originally, Tony and Mike were supposed to take the wrap for Booker's murder. They were the only ones who knew Oliver's real involvement. He'd planned to drop enough clues for investigators to easily connect the dots and build a case against them. Motive and planning? Clear as day.

But with that option no longer usable, he went with the next best choice: Miteous, who he had *no* problem framing.

He implemented the contingency plan the second he saw how the scene had unfolded between Tay, Tony, Mike, and Miteous. Once he spotted Miteous pick up that gun and head off with purpose, he knew revenge was on his mind, and all roads would lead him straight to the pawnshop.

So, Oliver waited.

Watching from a distance, seeing Miteous show up and walk right up to the front of the pawnshop was like watching a lamb walk to the slaughter.

He adjusted his high-tech spyware camera and snapped a couple photos, ones he planned to send anonymously. He had Miteous dead to rights the moment he saw him pick up the gun.

That's when Oliver decided to move things along.

He pulled out his burner phone and dialed 9-1-1.

"Emergency operator, how may I assist you?" the dispatcher asked.

"Yes, I was driving by the pawn shop downtown when I saw what looked like a break-in. I don't know what's going on, but I saw someone go in through the front, there's broken glass everywhere. Could you send a unit to check it out? I used to know the guy who owned the place a while ago," Oliver said, trying not to sound like himself, more like a concerned citizen passing through.

"No problem. Thank you for your call. We are sending additional units to that location now. And what is your name, sir?" the dispatcher asked.

But Oliver had already hung up.

Not wanting to compromise his positioning or alibi, he headed toward his next location, where he'd already set everything up. He could prove where he was during the time of the killings if he ever came under suspicion.

What he *wasn't* planning on, though, was the whole thing backfiring…

Because what Oliver lacked in his old age, was imagination.

Gun in hand, Miteous crept through the corridors. Something in him was telling him to get out of there again, but he kept going. When he crossed the threshold into Booker's office, he froze.

Booker was slumped behind his desk, lying in a pool of blood. Lifeless.

Dead from a gunshot wound.

Miteous had no idea how he got taken out, or who beat him there. But now he felt completely exposed and uncomfortable.

Thoughts racing, heart pounding, he damn near jumped out of his skin when the phone in Booker's office rang out of nowhere.

Caught completely off guard by the whole scene, head spinning from the trauma of so much recent death, Miteous picked up the receiver without thinking.

"You might wanna get outta there, lil nigga. First-degree murder with the use? Long time to be doin' on a plantation, even with time on yo side 'cause of how young you is, which is more than I can say about yo boy and that old-ass nigga on the other side of that desk. Consider this a common courtesy," the anonymous caller said.

Then they hung up.

Miteous's heart dropped into the pit of his stomach, not just from hearing the real killer's voice, but because he realized…

He'd just been set up.

And now he was caught *dead to rights.*

Literally, with the smoking gun in his hand.

Not even five minutes after returning the receiver to its base, Miteous heard sirens in the distance, closing in fast. All he could do was be mad at himself for not listening to his instincts… the God in him, warning him of the dangers ahead.

Pressed for time now, anxiety through the roof, he struggled to figure out how to navigate a situation like this. He tried putting on his thinking cap and started improvising, going with whatever came to mind that made the most logical sense.

Pulling the .357 from the small of his back, he walked over to Booker's dead body and placed the chrome revolver in the palm of his cold, stiff hand. Then he elevated Booker's body just enough and fired a single shot at the doorway, splinters of wood flying through the hall.

He turned to leave, wiping his prints off the gun he'd picked up earlier and tossing that one too, thinking if he was going to be charged for something he didn't do, then at least it wouldn't look the way the real killer had staged it. Maybe that'd give him a fighting chance… some kind of relief.

Exiting out the same front door he came in, he wasn't surprised to see twenty uniformed officers had the whole place surrounded. All he could do now was comply with their demands if he didn't want to be the next one shot.

"Freeze! Don't move! Get down on the ground! Hands interlocked behind your head, now!"

"Asshole," Officer Meales Davis muttered. He was head of the Major Crimes Division, now acting lead detective on this case. He specialized in burglary, murder, and kidnapping, had over twenty years on the job, and had served in four tours for his country, a real naval man, through and through.

He approached the scene looking like a character out of *The Godfather,* like he'd already pulled two doubles before showing up to work this one.

"I ain't do nothin', man! I'm bein' set up!" Miteous yelled in his defense from underneath a cop's boot as they brought him to his feet and cuffed him.

He was passed off from one officer to the next, each one asking the last if he'd been searched and cleared, while the detective was being briefed by one of the higher-ranking officers.

Eventually, Miteous was taken to a squad car and placed in the back until they figured out who he was, and what they were going to do with him.

After over an hour in the back of the car, the lead detective finally approached for an unofficial conversation. Miteous had been watching officers talk in circles, comparing notes and trying to make sense of what they *thought* happened, hoping they could use it as leverage in a real interview.

"What's up, man. How you doin'? I'm Detective Meales Davis, and I'm in charge of this investigation, you understand? Now let's just start with your name, young man," Officer Meales said through the lowered window.

"My name Miteous Reese," Miteous replied, ignoring the first question entirely. His mood made it clear: he already knew he was screwed.

"Okay, Miteous. You look pretty young. How old are you?" Meales asked, trying to get a feel for who he was dealing with, and to ease him into talking.

"I'm sixteen. I will be seventeen in a couple months," Miteous said, nothing more, nothing less, which seemed to slightly frustrate the detective.

"Well… what's goin' on here, man? Why'd we find you down here, this time of morning, with a dead guy in the back, multiple firearms around, and you comin' out the front door that was shattered from a gunshot?" Meales said, voice and tone suddenly shifting. He was done easing in, now he wanted answers.

"I came down here to get some answers… about what happened to my friend that was killed earlier today. Tay Vaughn Kelly. He used to work for this dude," Miteous replied with genuine sadness in his voice.

Something in his honesty hit Meales hard.

He quickly scrambled for his pen and notepad, jotting down what Miteous had just said. He now knew it was imperative to get his parents on the phone and bring him downtown for an official statement.

Having worked the homicides Miteous was referring to earlier, Meales was excited at the possibility of a lead. Hearing that all four murders might be connected through a common denominator could be huge.

He couldn't believe this kid was still alive through it all, and he was eager to find out exactly what Miteous knew.

Even though he had him exactly where he wanted him and might be one step closer to solving this whole thing and closing his cases, he still had to follow the law.

"Okay, sit tight, Miteous. We gon' get you down to the station. But first, I gotta read you your rights."

He pulled out a card and read:

"You have the right to remain silent. Anything you say or do can be used against you in a court of law. You have the right to an attorney. If you cannot afford one, one will be appointed for you. After hearing your rights, do you still wish to speak to me about what happened to your friend, or what's going on here today?"

Meales pulled out his cellphone, ready to dial.

"I don't know if that'd be in my best interest right now, officer," Miteous said, thinking hard for the first time since Tay got shot.

"Well then, what's your parents' number? Law says I can't talk to you without one of 'em present anyway," Meales replied.

Unfortunately, Miteous gave up the contact. His parents quickly agreed to meet them downtown at the station. And he already knew, they were going to be *pissed.*

They had no idea what he'd been mixed up in. And now that everything was about to hit the fan, it was time for some uncomfortable conversations.

Because this wasn't a game anymore.

He realized that if things went all the way left, the consequences weren't going to be temporary. No more being grounded. No more just getting sent to his room.

He could end up spending the rest of his life in prison.

Staring out the squad car window on the way to the station, Miteous had a lot on his mind. But the main thing was that phone call that came in *right* before the cops showed up.

And the one question burning in his head:

Who the hell was that mystery man? And how did he get the drop on me like that...?

"Ninety-seven... ninety-eight... ninety-nine... one hundred."

The six-foot, two-hundred-eighty-pound, musclebound killer named Tex counted out loud in his cell, finishing his last set of pushups. He hit a thousand a day, like clockwork.

Recovering to his feet, he went over to the sink attached to his toilet. That told you exactly where he was in life.

He splashed water on his face to wash the sweat, grabbed a mini towel, soaked it with soap, and started wiping his armpits and chest, getting ready for lunch. It usually showed up at the same time each day. And when it did, the inmates came together like loud kids, always rushing things and complaining.

Tex was mid-thought when two unexpected messages came to his door.

The first was a thick manila envelope, legal docs about his case from his lawyer. He tossed it on the bed. Wasn't in the mood for bad news right now.

The second was from a staff member who told him he had a clergy visit. A chaplain had come to see him in the private clergy room.

Tex changed into a clean jumpsuit and made his way down, having to wait at every hallway corner like a kindergarten kid. He hated that part.

Once he got there, he had to wait again, figuring they were clearing the visitor through the system.

He sat there waiting... then it finally hit him.

He didn't know *any* chaplains.

Hadn't stepped foot in a church since he was ten years old, back when his grandmother passed.

And that was the only reason he ever went in the first place.

So, when the man finally came in and started presenting himself as a religious coordinator, Tex immediately demanded to know what he wanted.

He wasn't trying to hear any of it.

He thought it might've been some impostor trying to trick him into some kind of confession.

"Now, I know we have never met before, my brother," the man started, "but everything is a part of God's plan and happens on His time, whether we choose to accept it or not. And the reason that brings us here today, together, although tragic, has also been uniting. We don't have to accept those terms either."

"A tragic one? Man, whatchu talkin' 'bout?" Tex replied, already thinking this dude was trying to convert him.

Now sitting forward in his seat, the man continued:

"I was told you were never fully made aware of this, Mr. Kelly… but you had a son. And he was just murdered last night."

Tex, who'd killed over a dozen people in his past, had never felt this low in his life. Not even close.

Afterward, when he returned to his cell, it didn't feel like a cell anymore, it felt like a tomb.

He'd just found out, for the first time, that he had a son. And that his son was killed before he ever got the chance to even know he existed. A son who probably felt abandoned… not knowing Tex never even knew he was alive.

Sitting on the edge of his bunk with his head down, all Tex could do was think back on the old days and ask himself one question:

How the hell did I let this happen?

Considering his line of work, and everything that came with it, Tex couldn't figure out who in their right mind would've ever gotten pregnant by him. Everybody knew what he did, even if they couldn't prove it. He was like a real-life John Wick.

But then, he remembered…

There was only one woman who ever really captured his heart. His high school sweetheart, Resheeda Brown.

She'd gotten hooked on drugs shortly after they graduated. Tex never thought her body could even carry a baby. And shortly after that, he got called overseas for work and lost touch.

But now… it had to be her.

She must've put him on the birth certificate. He didn't remember signing it himself. But now that the boy was gone, and that opportunity ripped from him, he was gonna make damn sure the person responsible *felt* that pain.

And even though he never knew he had a son, Tex was already plotting revenge.

For the first time in a long time, Tex hit his knees and prayed. Prayed to God that things went his way in court. Because now, on top of his current cases, he had unfinished business, business *only he* could attend to.

Head full of steam, eyes closed, he bowed his head and silently prayed…

For his enemies.

Back at headquarters, Miteous was placed in a small interview room, handcuffed to the table while he waited for his parents to arrive.

He was offered a snack and a drink. After he finished, he studied the room a bit more and noticed a small hidden camera in the top corner. He knew whatever he said next, they could play it back later and catch him in any lies.

So, he planned to be real careful, not to incriminate himself.

He also knew these detectives had been working multiple homicide cases they believed were all connected to Booker's spot. So, he needed to give them as little as possible while finding out how much they thought they already knew.

Just then, Officer Meales walked in, with Miteous's mom a few steps behind him.

She locked her gaze on him immediately, *that look.*

"Boy… what the hell you got yourself into now?"

She didn't say a word. But that look said everything. She didn't come in yelling or crying. She came in quiet, just waiting to be informed what her son had gotten caught up in.

And when she found out?

She still didn't say much.

But if a picture was worth a thousand words, then the look on Miteous's mom's face at that police station was worth a *whole* library. Because if *she* was at a loss for words? That was a real problem.

She got paid to talk for a living.

The witnesses couldn't account for Miteous's whereabouts after the party up until Tay was shot. Besides the two girls they were with before they left to get the car, it had only been him and Tay.

And he wasn't sure how strong an alibi either girl could give.

He'd just found out Patrese's uncles' names, and he was now certain *they* were the shooters. But he knew they weren't gonna flip on Booker and say he ordered the hit. That wasn't happening.

So, he didn't even bring them up.

Then there was the fact that he couldn't explain why they left the party without the girls they came with. He didn't want to incriminate himself with a grand theft auto charge, or *any* additional felonies.

Even though the officer kept saying he only cared about the homicides, Miteous felt like it was a trap. Like the detective was trying to bait him, hook him, and drop him in his tackle box.

And sure enough, that's when the script flipped.

Officer Meales tried telling Miteous he believed *he* killed Tay.

Said Tay had become a liability.

Said Miteous couldn't trust him anymore with their dirty little secrets.

He kept going and going…

Until Miteous killed the whole theory with one sentence.

"We showed up to that party with matching chains, dawg. The one he died in. That chain was a symbol of our bond. These wasn't no Halloween props or somethin' out the flea market."

The detective couldn't argue with that. So, he moved on to his next theory.

A couple hours passed, the detective going back and forth with questions. Then he got a message on his phone, checked it, and told Miteous and his mom he had something to show them. Said he'd be right back.

About twenty minutes later, he returned with a thick manila folder.

Once Officer Meales had their full attention, he started pulling out contents of the file, right in front of Miteous and his mother.

The first picture was of Miteous and Tay entering Booker's pawnshop a week ago.

Then he pulled out another one.

Alibimac. Dead at his tire shop.

"Do you know this guy?" Officer Meales asked.

Miteous answered honestly.

"Nah. I never seen him before. Why?"

And he hadn't. Not before that day, anyway.

"We'll come back to that," Meales said, still digging.

The next few photos were from the scene around the corner from where Tay was killed.

And the car Miteous had seen parked near it...

Now he was sure, it was Tony and Mike's.

When Miteous saw that, he started fidgeting in his seat.

Extremely uncomfortable.

The detective noticed right away.

"Do you know who all these folks had in common, young man?" Officer Meales asked rhetorically, tone full of patronizing heat.

"No, I do not, sir," Miteous said sarcastically, figuring the detective was gonna tell him what he thought anyway, so why not just play along.

"Well, son, if you've been paying any attention to my little presentation here, all these people had you and Montel Williams in common. AKA Booker. And now he's dead. We find you at the crime scene... and then there's this, which came in about an hour ago."

Officer Meales pulled out his final piece of evidence, a still shot of Miteous entering the front of the pawnshop with a gun in his hand, like he'd just blasted the door open.

"I'm bein' set up! Who took that picture anyway?! There was a phone call right before you guys showed up, I think it was the real killer. Check into that!" Miteous said, losing his composure. The five-hour interrogation was wearing him down, and this was the first time he realized they really had some evidence that could stick.

"Maybe," Meales said, shrugging. "But without an autopsy report, additional investigations, or witnesses… all I got is this, and you, to go off of for now, Mr. Reese. So, until there's proof otherwise, I got enough here to charge you with murder and use of a weapon to commit a felony."

He stood up, pulling out his handcuffs.

"And unfortunately, I gotta place you under arrest at this time and book you into the county jail until further notice."

Centering his Chi, Tex finally found a calm enough headspace to move through his day with some peace of mind.

After chow, he finished his meal, wandered around the unit a bit to be alone, and let his thoughts drift back to his childhood.

He thought about how his father had abandoned him, and now, here he was, part of the same cycle. Another young Black man out here who had to grow up without his father.

Even though he hadn't meant to add to that horrible statistic, not being careful where he planted his seed ended up being the same damn thing.

Growing up on the South Side of Chicago made him tough. Taught him how to survive in the trenches. But it was the mistakes he made in the streets that made him a man.

Tex was born Adam Kelly, and moved to Houston, Texas when he was eight years old to live with his grandparents after his mother got real sick. They were old, and even though they meant well, they couldn't keep up with him.

After his grandmother passed, the streets took him.

Tex committed his first murder at just eleven years old.

He'd been selling weed for a local dealer named Scooby, who had plenty of enemies and a long reach in the streets. Scooby used young kids to move weight, and when he saw little Tex roughing up some older kids on the blacktop one summer, he saw his heart, his fearlessness, and offered him a job.

Tex gladly accepted.

One day, Tex was moving a little shipment, just a couple pounds in a backpack, when he got robbed by some older guy. Tex went straight to Scooby to let him know what happened.

Scooby handed him a gun and said:

"Go get my shit back… or keep that for protection. Either way, you gon' need it."

After that, it was on.

Tex kept his ear to the streets and tracked the guy down to an old shipyard he knew well. He waited for his moment. Then, when he caught him slipping alone one day, he stepped out the shadows, shot him in the legs, pistol-whipped him, made him give up the stash… found triple what was taken… took it all…

…and killed him.

All in the same day.

That's when he earned the name Tex because that's where he got his start. And he became known for shortening people's lives, like an abbreviation.

He went on to do more murders for hire and made a career out of killing. His efficiency and relentlessness had his name floating in every major circle. He started getting recruited by big wigs to eliminate their competition. He became highly recommended and highly wanted.

So, whenever things got too hot, he moved.

State to state.

Eventually, he landed in Nebraska by high school, staying with his aunt. He thought it'd be a quiet place to finish school while the heat died down.

That's when he met Rasheeda.

First time he ever felt love.

They had a deep connection, and he really thought she was gonna be *the one*, until she got hooked on drugs and became someone he didn't even recognize anymore.

He graduated. Left. Never looked back.

Didn't know she got pregnant.

Didn't know she had a kid.

Didn't know he was even possibly the father.

Not until now.

Cleaning up his cell a little, Tex was still lost in thought. Then he remembered, he'd gotten mail earlier from the courts. Tired of dragging it out, he decided to open it. He wasn't hoping for much. In fact, his mind was already bracing for the worst.

He grabbed the manila envelope off his bed, tore it open, and read the first page inside.

It was a letter from the judge and prosecuting attorney on his case.

Dear Mr. Kelly,

You were scheduled for a hearing this month, but it is our duty to inform you that there have been new developments with your case. It is now under further review. A confidential informant, who was presented as the state's witness against you, has been killed and is no longer available at this time. The court is motioning for a dismissal without further prejudice...

CHAPTER 16

Waking up, making a cold bowl of cereal, then watching the morning news, that was his daily routine. He'd been doing it for so long, it was more like a ritual by now.

Crossing the living room to grab the remote, he turned on the TV and cranked the volume so he could hear it from the kitchen, about twenty feet away in his one-bedroom apartment, while he prepared breakfast and got his day started.

Even though he owned the whole building, unbeknownst to anybody else, his small but suitable living space was all he felt he needed. A reflection of his humility as a man.

But when Melvin Andrews heard the breaking news story come on *this* particular morning, everything changed.

He said to hell with that bowl of cereal and rushed back to the living room, eyes locked on the TV screen as his favorite anchorman read the script, calm voice, full of sympathy and compassion, detailing a tragic set of events from the night before.

Multiple people dead.

One person arrested.

And everything about it seemed suspicious.

"Authorities say it was after a late-night house party when the first shooting occurred, just blocks away from the residence, leaving one man dead from several gunshot wounds.

Then, not even a half hour later, police were called to another location where gunfire was reported again, just a few blocks away from the first scene. There, they found two more men dead inside a vehicle from several apparent gunshot wounds.

While investigating those shootings for a possible connection, officers were dispatched hours later to a break-in at a downtown pawn shop, where another man was found dead.

Police arrested a teenage boy still on scene, who they believe may be linked to the previous incidents. At this time, authorities have declined to comment further, saying the investigation is still ongoing.

Whether these events are connected and whether the teen is being charged with all four homicides is yet to be determined.

This is a developing story. We'll continue to update as we receive new details.

If you've seen or heard anything, the police are urging community members to come forward to help solve these cases. If you'd like to remain anonymous, please contact our hotline. And if your information leads to an arrest, you could receive a cash reward.

I'm Matthew Jacobs, reporting live, Channel 9 News. Now we'll go to Hailey with your weather forecast for the week."

That's when Melvin started putting the pieces together in his head.

Based on what he knew, and who he knew had been involved, everything started pointing to one name: Oliver Maxwell.

It had his signature written all over it.

Even though he didn't have any proof yet, Melvin had served under Oliver's command for years. He knew exactly how the man operated, left nothing to chance, always tied up loose ends. There was always a fall guy. And all the evidence? It always pointed *somewhere else.*

Melvin had only one advantage now, one thing going in his favor to finally take the drop on Oliver:

Nobody even knew who he really was.

Nobody knew where he really lived. He'd changed his name after leaving the military... then changed it *again* when he started working with the feds.

Only Randy and Mike knew who he really was, and that's only because they'd known each other from way back.

Nobody knew that Melvin's real name used to be Phillip.

Nobody knew he'd been set up by Oliver.

Nobody knew his little brother had been killed after the war.

Nobody knew he went to the feds, got out rich, and had been working as a correctional officer in the county jail for years, waiting on the perfect moment to get revenge on everyone involved in the conspiracy.

So, when he saw Booker's empire falling apart right in front of him, he couldn't wait. He grabbed his things, got dressed, and headed out, ready to report to his shift supervisor.

Excited.

Because it was finally time to start moving on his own plans, one's nobody would see coming.

After all, how do you defend yourself against an enemy you don't even know you have?

Right before Officer Meales escorted Miteous out of the station, he turned to his mother.

"I'm sorry... and I love you. Don't worry, I'm innocent," he told her.

And she believed him.

He carried himself with strength, the same strength she'd instilled in him growing up. He kept his head high, even in chains.

Seeing them escort her baby boy out like that, shackled up for something she knew he didn't do, was painful. But she held it together. Put on a poker face, just like he did.

They parted without tears. Only steel in their eyes.

At that moment, all Miteous could think was, where was his father?

Normally, he figured he was at work. But now… maybe he was too embarrassed to show up. Maybe he couldn't face him.

Maybe.

And even if that *wasn't* the case, Miteous understood why it might've been. So, he let the thought go, refocused, and started preparing his mind for whatever came next.

After collecting his DNA samples, fingerprints, and personal clothing, the officers tried one last time to coerce him into a confession.

He stayed silent.

They snapped his mugshot, then threw him in the back of a squad car and drove him to county jail.

Walking into county jail through the garage felt like entering a slaughterhouse.

The officers locked up their weapons in secure lockers, then escorted Miteous inside to be processed.

It was like walking into an airport to book a flight straight to hell.

People everywhere, coming and going, getting moved in and out of holding cells. Yelling. Screaming. Young. Old. In-between.

Didn't matter the age, race, or background.

They all had one thing in common.

Everybody in there had been arrested for *something*.

Finding out indictments were on the way left Oliver Maxwell with no other choice.

Booker had allowed himself to be infiltrated. Not just by people outside the organization, but by folks inside it too.

So, Oliver made a decision.

"Better to cut off an arm or leg than let the whole-body rot," he told himself.

That was his mentality.

His plan?

Operation: Gangrene.

And if he hadn't hired Melvin when he did, he would've never been watching his back so closely. Never noticed how so many things around him weren't adding up.

Taking a closer look into his own crew, he discovered something that made his blood go cold.

Christopher Evans. AKA Alibimac.

He'd been pulled over six months ago in a traffic stop. Cops found several ounces of crack and a loaded firearm.

They took everything but never charged him.

Alibimac walked away scot-free after a lengthy interview and agreed to become a confidential informant and wear a wire on Booker.

Then he found out from a close friend, still reporting to a desk in his old line of work, that the feds had flipped one of his old army sergeants. Word was, dude had started talking about some old war crimes, stuff linked to human trafficking overseas, and so Oliver had to shut him up, too.

But the strange thing about the situation with Randy… Oliver just couldn't figure out why, after all these years, Randy chose now to switch up on him. Especially knowing damn well Oliver could still get to him. Even though Randy was a little off, Oliver had made sure Booker set him up sweet when he got back to the States, had him running illegal firearms to the city's most organized gangs, making sure Randy never wanted for anything. So why bite the hand that fed him?

Either way, it was Randy's decision. One he chose to live with, and one he ended up dying by. Not knowing Randy was never in it for the money. That he'd always wanted to take Oliver down by any means necessary. And he'd risked his life in the process just to try and stop the big bad wolf…

Once Tex finally calmed down, after getting that high off life that only the dead coming back to life could ever feel, he went straight for the attorney's number. Then sprinted into the dayroom to use the jail phone.

"Robert Jones Attorney Office, how may I help you?" His female secretary answered sweet and polite.

"Yeah, may I speak with Robert?" Tex said, pacing hard, the metal phone cord stretched out from the wall like it was about to snap from his excitement and anxiety.

"No, he's not available right now," she replied. "I was told he stepped out to visit some clients. May I leave a message?"

"Um, nah. That's okay. Thanks anyway," Tex said, then hung up, his head spinning in anticipation of the visit.

A few hours later, his attorney finally came to see him. And Tex lit up like a puppy waiting all day on its owner to get home.

He was already in the private visitation room, happy to see Robert waiting on him instead of the other way around like usual.

"Hey. How you doin' today, Mr. Kelly?" Robert Jones said, diplomatic as always.

He was a wiry old white dude, used to be in shape back in his prime when he played quarterback for Indiana. But that was ages ago. Now he was just trying to retire in one piece after over twenty years practicing law, which had earned him both enemies and powerful connections.

"I'd be a whole lot better once you give me some news I can use," Tex replied, all business now, ready to cut through the B.S.

"Well, I'm not gonna sit here and bullshit you, man. It's pretty bad, this hole you've dug yourself into. You might've just caught a break on this one here due to a technicality, no doubt. But the one in Virginia? You ain't gettin' outta that one easy, my friend."

He paused, then leaned in slightly, lowering his voice.

"But lucky for you... I know a few people. And the bottom line is, the state and the feds both want these recent murders solved. It's got folks panicking. So, if you scratch their back, they're willing to scratch yours."

Tex's eyes narrowed. "And what exactly you talkin' 'bout?"

"Simple," Robert said, with that crooked-ass smile of his. "All they want you to do is try and get this young kid to open up to you. If you can get him to talk about what happened, you walk. Debt paid. Services rendered."

"Alright, man. Fuck it. What other choice do I got? What's the kid's name? And who'd he kill anyway?"

"His name's Miteous. And he's headed here now, probably being processed as we speak. Just sit out these hundred-and-twenty failure-to-appears for sixty days, and I'll get you time served. Plenty of time to work the kid."

Robert leaned back in his chair.

"I already told 'em you ain't wearin' no wire or nothin'. But they'll only grant your freedom with a full confession, and it's gotta match their evidence, so we need specifics."

Tex wasn't no snitch. Never had been. But if there was one thing he did know, it was how to manipulate the system. Whatever deal he had to make with the devil to get his freedom back, he was gonna make sure it worked in his favor.

He signed the agreement the prosecutor's office had already drawn up, ended the attorney visit, and was returned to his unit, ready to wait for the next guest fate was about to bring his way.

When Melvin clocked in for work, they told him to report to admissions since they were short on staff. He made his rounds and saw there were several people waiting to be processed, so he decided to handle it himself.

The first person he changed out of regular clothes into the county-issued jumpsuit seemed like he'd been there before. Dude already knew the drill before Melvin even had to say anything.

Then in came this young kid, barely even looked old enough to be in the county with the grown folks.

Once Melvin found out who he was, he helped him out immediately.

"Ay, you that lil nigga they booked for smokin' Booker, ain't you?" Melvin asked.

"Yeah, but I ain't do that shit. He was already dead when I got there," Miteous replied, like he'd said it a thousand times, but nobody ever believed him.

"I know he was. I was in the military with a nigga that really smoked 'em," Melvin said, giving Miteous a look like they were the only two in the world who knew the truth, and something wasn't right about this whole setup.

"But how did you? I ain't never seen you around before. Who are you?" Miteous asked, thrown off.

"My name Melvin. I was in the game too with all dem fools till they double-crossed me. Had my brother killed and sent me to the feds for twenty years. So, I know what you goin' through. Listen to me, this all a setup. Don't trust nobody. Don't talk to nobody. I got a plan."

He handed Miteous his state-issued clothing. But when Miteous grabbed it, he felt something hard in the middle of the jumpsuit.

When he went to get dressed, he found it, a small cell phone, about the size of his palm. Easy to conceal.

"Put that in a sock and tie it 'round yo' nuts, young homie. Then wait to hear from me," Melvin said as he dipped out to make sure everything else was lining up just right.

Miteous walked out of admissions with more hope than he had before. He didn't know how things were gonna play out, but one thing he knew now, he wasn't alone in this fight.

He had somehow gained an ally. Someone who apparently had a common enemy. Because for somebody to know he didn't kill Booker... they had to want the real killer just as bad.

And if that meant Miteous had to help him get to that person? Then so be it.

He wasn't in no position to turn down a helping hand. Even if it meant being collateral damage.

That still beats spending the rest of his life in prison.

After getting dressed, concealing his lifeline, and being seen by a nurse for any medical needs, Miteous was escorted by staff to his new housing unit, F mod.

Once there, they directed him to his assigned cell. When he got there, he saw one of the biggest dudes he'd ever seen in real life.

Guy looked like a straight-up Green Mile John Coffey type.

"Wassup man, my name Miteous. They assigned me to this cell. That ain't gon' be a problem, is it?" he asked.

"Yeah, I know. It's all good. Top bunk's yours, young homie. Make yo'self at home. I'm Adam. Adam Kelly…"

EPILOGUE

The devil's greatest trick was convincing the world he didn't even exist. Because if you don't know who your real enemy is, how can you ever prepare a proper defense or predict their next move? That was just one of many lessons Miteous Reese had to learn the hard way.

Walking through the hallways of the county jail, arrested for a murder he didn't commit, Miteous could feel the phone in the sock tied around his private area loosening with every step. He'd just gotten it from his newfound ally, Melvin Phillips, who happened to work intake and somehow knew more about Miteous's situation than he did at that point.

He kept having to adjust it with awkward movements, making sure it didn't fall down his pant leg before he reached his destination. That phone was a valuable resource, one that might just put him a step closer to getting his freedom back.

Entering through a set of manually controlled sliding doors that led to his assigned housing unit for the first time, Miteous didn't know what to expect. But the feeling that came over him when he stepped onto the gallery floor and looked around, he couldn't even put it into words.

All eyes were on him.

Instant paranoia set in. He was in an unsettling environment surrounded by grown men who clearly outmatched him in size and experience. His mind shifted to defense, how he'd hold his own if it came to a fight, but no good ideas came. His thoughts spiraled, racing a hundred miles per hour.

Trying to calm his nerves, he took a few deep breaths and started assessing the situation.

His hands were full, carrying his interchangeable state-issued clothing and bedroll. He had no real way to defend himself if someone tried to test him about the charges he'd been hit with. The more he thought about it, the more exposed he felt. So, he decided to find his assigned cell as fast as possible to set his stuff down and free up his hands, just in case.

Everything that had gone down over the last seventy-two hours still hadn't hit him fully. But now it started to sink in, he was facing a life sentence. Just a few days ago, he had a bright future. Now? He had enemies coming for him, people he didn't even know. He didn't know what they looked like, who they were connected to, or even if they were in the same unit with him.

And then there were the victims' families. What they were capable of, who they knew, he had no idea. For all he knew, they had folks in the very same housing unit he'd been assigned to.

As soon as he processed that thought, he stopped and began scanning his surroundings like Tay had taught him, trying to pick up on any immediate threats through body language and demeanor. But there was just too much going on for his underdeveloped instincts to catch anything real.

He was walked over to a desk posted up on a high-rise, like a toll booth. That's where the corporals sat, pressing the buttons that controlled the doors. Once they looked him up and gave him his cell number, he started heading in that direction.

What he hadn't noticed was that he wasn't the only one walking toward that cell, and by the time he did, it was too late.

A massive man was closing in from behind.

When Miteous got to the cell and went to set his stuff down, he saw there were bunk beds in every room. The bottom bunk had already been claimed, so he had to take the top. As he moved to drop his things on the rubber mat, he noticed he almost set it right in a puddle of water.

That's when it hit him, he was in danger. This was a setup.

He spun around and dropped everything he was holding. Standing in the doorway was a heavyset, dark-skinned dude with a scruffy beard and a smirk on his face. There was a real dark energy about him.

"Ay, you that lil nigga that was just on the news? Down for that shit at the pawn shop downtown, ain't chu?" he asked, voice filled with tension.

Then, outta nowhere, he rushed Miteous, throwing closed-fist punches as soon as he was close enough.

All Miteous could do was defend himself. He was caught completely off guard by how quick it all went down, but he kept his guard up and swung back when he had the chance.

After a few moments of scrapping with the oversized behemoth, corporals stormed in, broke it up, cuffed them both, and dragged them out the unit.

Miteous was taken to a different part of the facility, checked out by medical staff, and then transferred to a whole other unit, placed on lockdown by himself for the rest of the night.

Sitting in that empty cell alone, fresh off that fight, that first night in jail hit him like a ton of bricks. He'd never felt so low in spirit. Everything that could go wrong had gone wrong, and he was still trying to process all the raw emotion built up inside.

It felt like everything that ever meant something to him was falling apart right before his eyes, and he couldn't do a damn thing to stop it. Honestly, death would've felt less painful.

For the first time in a long time, Miteous dropped to his knees and prayed to God. Called on the Most High, Creator of the universe, to take over the direction of his life. Poured his heart out, heavy with sin and survivor's guilt. And he meant every word.

He thanked Him for sparing his life in situations he knew he shouldn't have survived. Then he surrendered all power and control, everything he thought he had in his hands, and asked God to fight his battles. Because He was the only one who could guarantee victory now.

He begged for forgiveness. Asked to be shown the way. And he prayed like that all night until he was so tired, he didn't even notice when he'd fallen asleep.

Thankful he hadn't been asked to strip search again. Thankful the lifeline Melvin gave him was still on him. Thankful to still have a little hope left.

Miteous didn't know how he'd gotten there, but now he was behind the wheel of a 1995 BMW, the same one Mike Epps drove on *Next Friday*. The sun was shining and judging by the bags on the passenger side floor, he'd just come from the corner store.

He recognized the street he was on. He must've been heading home.

The more comfortable he got behind the wheel, the faster he started driving. Turned down a couple backstreets and hit a dirt road he used all the time as a shortcut; it led straight to the block he lived on.

But what he didn't know was, ever since he'd left that store, he'd been followed.

And the wild, erratic driving style he'd developed over time, like he was in a *Mario Kart* race, was now the very thing that was saving his life. It bought him just enough time to make a critical decision.

When he finally pulled up to his house, the driveway was full, so he parked on the street. He sat there for a few minutes, thinking about what he wanted to do once he got inside.

Then outta nowhere, he got a strange feeling in his gut.

Something was telling him to get out the car.

But he ignored it.

216

A few minutes later, when he finally decided to open the door…

He couldn't.

Because of how the traffic started to come.

First, a car turned onto his narrow street, which didn't even have sidewalks, preventing him from opening his door safely. It sped up the block on the opposite side, making him pay attention to any other cars coming or going. Then he saw that car pass another one that was headed down on his same side. Now he was really at the mercy of oncoming traffic and had to wait for them to pass as well.

Except, when this car came down his street and got to where his vehicle was parked at, it pulled up right next to him and stopped.

Surprised by the sudden maneuver, Miteous couldn't do anything but wait to see what they were on or what they'd do next, because he was officially boxed in. The only way out was crawling over to the passenger side, which was a long shot in those tight spaces, but he definitely should've done it if he'd known he was in immediate danger.

But he didn't know.

Not until they rolled down their window and he was staring face-to-glock, down the barrel of a gun held by an unknown assailant.

"You know what time it is, nigga!" the anonymous assailant yelled out, before he started blasting on Miteous over and over again.

And before he could even move or protest, Miteous was staring over at himself in the metaphysical. He was now just in Astro form, looking at his lifeless body slumped in the driver's seat of his car, like some twisted scene out of a Doctor Strange movie...

"Mr. Reese... Mr. Reese..." the corporal called from outside his cell door.

He came out of his deep slumber, dazed and confused, saw it was time to go and retrieve his breakfast from the cell door hatch, and realized it had all been just a bad dream. He silently thanked God for that, praying over his food before devouring it.

That's when the corporal doubled back to inform him that he'd just gotten word, he was gonna be moved again after breakfast. Another staff member was coming to escort him to his new housing unit. He needed to be ready to leave shortly.

And that was like music to his ears. Having just been a free man less than forty-eight hours ago, he was already going stir crazy being confined to that empty cell against his will. He couldn't figure out for the life of him how anybody got used to that over time, even if it was only because they didn't have a choice.

If this was how he was gonna have to live out the rest of his days until further notice, then he was definitely gonna need to find an outlet. Being caged like an animal for long periods of time was bound to drive him to his breaking point.

After finishing his meal and getting his hygiene together, he was seen by the corporal that handled all disciplinary actions. He was officially assigned back to the general population since they determined he hadn't done anything he wasn't supposed to.

He was told he'd be sent to F-Mod once a staff member was available to escort him.

About a half hour later, Miteous was escorted to his new housing unit. And once he got inside that new pod, he could tell, and feel, that things were gonna be totally different, just from the vibe alone.

It was like nobody was paying attention to what anyone else had going on. Everybody was all in their own world. Some folks were playing chess and cards. Others were on the phone with their people. Some watched the big screen TV posted up in the center of the unit, while others played a game of pickup basketball outside.

Everybody seemed older. And everybody was in their own lane.

As he walked through the unit and was directed to his new cell, he searched around until he found his corridor. But he was shocked when he got there and saw one of the biggest dudes he'd ever seen in person. Apparently, this was his new cellmate now. And after what he just went through, he was praying this dude was more on the friendly side, not another foe.

Completely uncomfortable walking into this new situation but not wanting to show any signs of weakness in the face of adversity, like he was taught, he decided to walk right up on the guy, try to get a feel for who he was by introducing himself first.

"Wassup, man. My name Miteous. They assigned me to this cell. That ain't gon' be a problem witchu, is it, big man?" he said assertively to the John Coffey off *Green Mile* lookalike.

"Yea, I know who you is. It's all good, young homie. Top bunk's yours. Make yo'self at home. I'm Adam, Adam Kelly," he replied calmly, extending his hand in a friendly manner.

After introducing himself, Miteous couldn't help but ask after shaking his hand, which felt like two of his put together.

"Kelly? How many other Kellys you know?" Miteous asked outta curiosity.

"I'm the only one out here. I'm from Texas, but all my peoples in Chicago carry the last name too. Why? Which ones do you know?" Tex replied, trying to keep the young man talking since he initiated the conversation.

"Well, I had a best friend named Tay Vaughn Kelly," he said innocently, unaware of the connection, with a hint of sadness in his voice.

"You know Tay?" Tex said enthusiastically, a totally different vibe now as his eyes widened in anticipation.

"Hell yea. Since kindergarten. Best friend in the world. And now..." Miteous replied but couldn't finish the sentence. He got too emotionally overwhelmed and started tearing up, almost breaking down for the second time since that tragic evening. He thought about those last moments with Tay that changed the course of his life forever, trying to hold back the pain, not wanting to cry in front of a complete stranger, especially under these circumstances.

"It's koo, young homie. I already know whatchu experiencing. I just dried my eyes from earlier, right before you walked in, lil man. I ain't even know I had a son until he was gone, because of his no-good-ass mama keepin' secrets and her addiction," Tex said, visibly upset, becoming vulnerable with Miteous for the first time, revealing to him that he was, indeed, the father of his slain best friend...

After Tex realized who Miteous really was and what was really going on, he knew exactly what he had to do now. And he knew exactly how to get it done too.

But first, he had to find out more info, get Miteous to trust him enough to reveal specifics about what he'd been into out there that got him in this position in the first place. So, he could use it to their advantage. So, he could get out of there, get revenge for his son's death, and free him in the process, knowing Miteous was gonna be the key.

Moreover, this first day couldn't have gone any better in his mind. Meeting Miteous for the first time and discovering that he was best friends with the only child he never got the chance to know? He saw it as a sign of fate. A blessing. Some good fortune that was meant to come from this connection.

He was now in the presence of the one person in the world who probably knew his son best and could tell him everything he wanted to know about him. Especially who killed him. Furthermore, all the key players Tay had been involved with out there and had been dealing with could've had some involvement too. Who knew what they were into while they'd been running together?

So, Tex had to make sure he was thorough. Had to leave no stone unturned when it came to doing his own little investigation. Had to inflict as much pain as humanly possible on all parties responsible, whoever had anything to do with it. Not to mention gathering all the vital information he'd need to turn his own situation around too.

Now he was really looking forward to getting to know Miteous better. But he could tell, just from talking to the young man briefly, that this was all gonna be easier said than done. Miteous wasn't your average teenage kid, he definitely had his wits about him, no matter how passive he came across.

This was gonna require a lot of finesse on his part, especially being in such a limited and restricted situation. But he still planned on executing his plans to the fullest, regardless. He wasn't about to end up just another one of those *woulda, coulda, shoulda* type people, stuck in prison forever, wishing they'd made better decisions when they had the chance.

No matter what...

Made in the USA
Middletown, DE
20 June 2025

77085723R00135